DATE DUE

| | | | |
|---|---|---|---|
| 11-26 | | | |
| | | | |
| | | | |
| | | | |
| | | | |
| | | | |
| | | | |
| | | | |
| | | | |
| | | | |
| | | | |
| | | | |

# LIGHT IN THE DARK

# LIGHT IN THE DARK

•

**Fran McNabb**

*AVALON BOOKS*
NEW YORK

Published by Thomas Bouregy & Co., Inc.
160 Madison Avenue, New York, NY 10016

Library of Congress Cataloging-in-Publication Data

McNabb, Fran.
Light in the dark / Fran McNabb.
p. cm.
ISBN 0-8034-9802-0 (acid-free paper)
I. Title.

PS3613.C5856L54 2006
813'.6—dc22

2006018079

PRINTED IN THE UNITED STATES OF AMERICA
ON ACID-FREE PAPER
BY HADDON CRAFTSMEN, BLOOMSBURG, PENNSYLVANIA

To my husband, Don, who never
let me forget my dream.

The beauty of the mountain ranges in West Virginia is unsurpassed. I hope the liberties I've taken with the topography, the parks, and the buildings in the southern part of the state are accepted for what this is: a work of fiction.

## *Chapter One*

Margaret Daniels stood in ankle-deep snow. Deep in thought, she broke a twig into tiny pieces, tossed each little segment into a stream inches from her feet, then watched them bob in the ripples before disappearing beneath the clear water.

Nothing disturbed the silence of the surrounding forest except the rippling water and an occasional rustling in the underbrush.

She closed her eyes and inhaled the clear mountain air. *This is exactly what I need. Finally, I can think.*

For as long as she could remember, she'd been coming to this park, first with friends of her parents, then with her husband. Now, with so much happening in the past few months, she needed this solitude.

She tossed the last twig into the water and headed toward her cabin to once again spend her Christmas vacation alone in the Southern Appalachian Mountain Range of West Virginia.

The familiar quaintness of the cabin, with its worn, mismatched furniture, warmed her as much as its huge fireplace would soon do. Right now only an electric heater threw off its heat from the corner of the room. At check-in Joe apologized for not having the wood waiting for her, but he'd assured her she'd have a blazing fire in her fireplace soon. Now too old to haul wood himself, he'd have someone else deliver it.

Before she had time to open her suitcase, the sound of crunching ice on the winding trail outside signaled the arrival of her firewood. She left the suitcase on the bed and answered the heavy knock at the door.

"Mrs. Daniels? I have a load of wood for you."

Margaret looked beyond the red plaid jacket to the logs in the truck. "Thank you. I was expecting it."

"Yeah, Joe wasn't going to be satisfied until I got these logs to you."

Margaret pulled her attention back to the man and looked up into a friendly smile. "That's just like Joe. He worries about me the whole time I'm up here."

The man glanced at the empty room behind Margaret. "He said you're up here alone. Is that true?"

Margaret hesitated. The man wasn't wearing a

park ranger uniform, but knowing Joe wouldn't send someone who couldn't be trusted, she nodded. "I come up here every year about this time—sort of a working vacation."

He backed up against the railing and pulled out a pack of gum, took one for himself, then offered her a stick.

"Thank you." How long had it been since she'd had a piece of gum?

"I'm Paul Reynor. Don't you get lonesome up here? I mean, it's none of my business, but this isn't the most desirable place to spend Christmas. It's perfect for chestnuts roasting on an open fire, but those yuletide carolers are going to have one heck of a time finding your cabin."

His eyes, the color of deep milk chocolate, twinkled as his face relaxed into a crooked grin.

Margaret smiled at his attempt to humor her. Probably in his early forties, he wore the look of a hard-working family man.

"You're right," she said deciding to go along with his mountain wit. "I don't get many carolers. I think it's the missing streetlight that's keeping them away."

He looked out at the snow-covered road, where a dented red truck sat next to her shiny sedan. "A streetlight would definitely help. Of course, a street wouldn't hurt either."

They both chuckled, then stood in the waning

daylight. It felt good to laugh, even if it had been a stranger who had unlocked that emotion. After hibernating for the past few weeks grading stacks of essays, Margaret felt a weight slip away.

Feeling comfortable in the man's presence, she leaned against the doorjamb and surprised herself by offering a bold invitation. "I haven't had time to make anything in the way of refreshments, but could I offer you a cup of hot chocolate for bringing the wood up to me?"

He looked at his watch. "That sounds good, but it's getting late."

Pushing aside a little sting of disappointment, she smiled. "I understand."

"I appreciate your offer, but I've got my sister and her family up for the weekend, and if I'm late, she'll worry. She's never gotten used to driving in the snow and thinks no one else should either. I'll haul this wood in for you and then get your fire started."

He pushed away from his railing, piled several logs in his arms, then strode past her. After taking several loads into the house and stacking another outside near her steps, he came back in and knelt by the fireplace. He arranged a small pile of kindling, then nursed a fire until it caught.

Satisfied that it would burn, he stood up and dusted his pants. "Keep close tabs on that basket of kindling. Don't let yourself run out."

"Thank you. I'll do that." Normally she wouldn't have asked anything personal of a stranger, but something about this man piqued her curiosity. "Do you live around here? I've been coming up here for years, but I don't think I remember seeing you before."

"I live south of here, not far, almost to the Virginia state line. Moved back last summer." He looked back at the fireplace. "I think I'll carry in some more logs for you."

"No need—" but he was already out the door.

Raising an eyebrow, she smiled at his take-charge attitude. Her Edward had also been a man in control, but his long, lean lines, suave dress, and scholarly manner left little else in common with Paul.

Still, something about Paul touched a chord deep in the center of her being. Margaret almost laughed out loud at that thought. She'd known the man less than five minutes. How could he strike anything within her?

She opened the door just in time for him to back through with another armful of wood. Small chips clung to the sleeve of his jacket. Without thinking, she reached out to remove a piece, but pulled her hand back before she embarrassed herself by touching a complete stranger. Thankful that he hadn't noticed her action, she let out a deep breath, then helped him stack the wood by the hearth.

Margaret knew she was probably in his way, but she enjoyed watching him toss the wood without any effort from the pile to the bin. He was meticulous, filling the bin to the rim, then picking up the fine chips that had fallen on the floor.

For the last couple of years since Edward's death, Margaret had accustomed herself to doing things on her own. Why she would get such pleasure from watching this man do such a menial thing puzzled her.

With the woodbin full, Paul stood up and brushed off his pants legs. "That ought to hold you."

She placed her hands on her knees to push herself up, but realized he'd held out his hand to help. For a moment she looked at his large hand. Even without touching him, she could see the calluses and toughened skin that made his hands so different from Edward's long, slender fingers.

Blinking to rid herself of the visual comparison, she placed her hand in Paul's. "Thank you. I guess the knees aren't what they used to be."

He helped her up, then stepped back. "I know what you mean. Mine are reminding me all too often about those times I hit the ground on the football field. Thought it was cool back then. Now I wish I'd been a little more careful."

"I imagine football can be pretty rough. I don't have that excuse, but my tennis game is starting to feel the results of old body parts."

He laughed out loud. "I don't think either of us fit into the *old* category. Well-used parts maybe, but that just means we didn't let life pass us by."

She smiled. "I'll have to tell myself that when I'm rubbing analgesics after my next set."

"I haven't played tennis since . . ." he thought a minute, "decades, I guess. That's a physical sport. I'm impressed."

"Well, don't be. I play in the women's doubles. None of us are very physical or very good, I might add. We just like to get out on the court and have fun."

"Don't cut yourself short. Any sport is good for the body and the soul. If it's something you really enjoy doing, well, that's even better. Life's too short not to do what we enjoy, isn't it?"

She nodded. That's exactly what she'd been telling herself lately. "I do enjoy being on the court with the ladies. It's a nice outlet for us."

He turned to go.

"I really do appreciate your doing all this." *And brightening my afternoon for these few minutes.* She looked toward the fire, not to have to look into his eyes. "I love to have a fire blazing. I think I miss that most in my apartment on campus."

He hesitated at the door. "You live on a college campus? Not the one in Bluefield, is it?"

"Yes, as a matter of fact, it is."

"Nice campus. I know it well. I'm living on the outskirts of town right now."

"When you said you lived near the state line, I wondered if that's where you meant. I'm surprised I haven't seen you around town." Even as she said the words, she knew that their worlds would probably never cross paths. Rarely did she leave campus except to visit colleagues, buy a few necessities, and to spend time in Boston with a few of her parents' friends. No, their paths would rarely have occasion to cross.

"I spend a lot of my time here at the park and at another lot I own."

"It's a nice town. I've been part of that campus for almost eleven years. I love it, and since it's not far from here, I can visit whenever I want. With no snow on the roads today, I made it up to the park in about thirty minutes."

"So you come up here a lot?"

"Not as much as I'd like, but I do get here during the holidays. It was a tradition my husband and I had."

"Nice tradition."

"Yes, it was, but we usually came up the week after Christmas."

"You and your husband lived on campus?"

"No, I moved to campus . . ." She didn't want to talk about Edward. Not today. "I moved there at the beginning of this semester. It's much more convenient than driving from out of town."

He stood quietly, and for a moment, Margaret thought maybe he wouldn't continue the conversation. Why should he? He had better things to do than to talk with a woman in a cabin. But then he surprised her.

"I guess it would be more convenient living next to your work, especially with the snows we've been having in the last few years. Probably a smart move on your part."

Smart move? That's what she'd thought when she sold the spacious two-story that she and Edward had been so proud of. Her campus apartment was convenient, efficient, and, if she were honest with herself, absolutely boring.

Paul stood with one dark eyebrow raised waiting for her answer.

She pulled herself back to the present. "Yes, I guess it was a smart move. It does keep me in touch with campus life, but I do miss our, uh, my house. I lived in the house for almost three years alone. I'm not sure what possessed me to sell last summer. Maybe it was the prospect of driving in all that snow again. When a realtor friend of mine suggested I sell, I stuck the For Sale sign up and within a month was moved into my apartment. It all happened so fast, I didn't have time to change my mind."

"I'm sure apartments are fine for some people, but I tried it once and hated it. Got to have my space. I'm renting right now, but I have a big yard that backs up to the woods and my other lot is about a mile from the nearest neighbor." His face broke out into a broad smile. "I've got the best of both worlds."

She didn't think hauling wood for park guests was part of an ideal world, but what did she know?

He reached for the door handle.

"You sure I can't fix you that cup of chocolate?"

This time he looked as though he was considering the offer, but instead shook his head. "It's tempting, but my sister'll have supper waiting, and I don't want to miss a home-cooked meal."

"I understand. It's not often I get a home-cooked meal either. It's easier to hit the campus deli."

This time he stepped outside the cabin but turned back to her. "Let Joe know if you need anything. I'll be back up here on Monday."

Pulling her jacket tight, she stood outside the door as he cranked his truck, waved, then disappeared around the curve. She stood on the stoop listening as the low roar of his truck grew fainter.

It was quiet. Too quiet. She looked up at the tree limbs hung heavy with snow then down at the tracks of Paul's truck that cut another new trail along the road away from her cabin. A horrible loneliness enveloped her. She stood in the fading light and stared at the tracks.

Where was the peace that this place normally brought her? This secluded cabin had always cheered her up, but as she looked out over the road once again, jabs of long-hidden desires stung her.

Silly that a complete stranger could remind her of what life no longer offered. She pulled her coat close to her body then stepped inside. Her suitcase still lay open on the bed. She looked longingly at the fire now blazing in the hearth, then frowned as she walked over to finish unpacking.

Piece by piece she pulled out the few necessities she'd brought, refolded them, and stacked them neatly in the same pine dresser she'd used for years. She wouldn't require much while she was here—a couple pairs of jeans, sweaters, and a few sets of lounging clothes.

Of course, there was always that one black dress she carried with her just in case she had to attend a function connected with the college. Shaking out the wrinkles, she hung it in the empty closet then placed her heels and black evening bag on the top shelf.

With her only chore for the evening completed, she warmed a can of soup, then sat in an old Boston rocker in front of the fire to enjoy her first night away from the hustle and bustle of campus life. For the next few weeks, she'd sit in front of this fireplace with her laptop and let the rest of the world zoom through the whirlwind of the holiday season.

She'd tried living through the first holidays in town without Edward, but putting on a façade of holiday cheer had been torturous. Her friends had included her in all their holiday get-togethers, but looking back, she now knew she hadn't been ready. It had only been three months earlier when Edward's heart had simply stopped working. His death had been quick and painless, a blessing for him, but agony for her.

She looked around the cabin. For the next two years she'd retreated here, alone, to avoid having to face the pain she'd faced that first holiday season. This year, though, the quiet of the mountains was more than an escape. It was a necessity. She had to have time alone to think about where her life was going.

Would she stay wrapped in the security of her small campus or would she step out to accept the job offer that had come in just before the semester ended?

Her life was starting to move again, but it was easier to watch the flames dance around the fireplace than to think about the decisions she'd have to make. The crackle of the fire made her think of Paul's comment about roasting chestnuts. The thought made her smile, but then she remembered what he'd said about not having any carolers and a moment of sadness settled around her once again.

During the holiday seasons, she and Edward had always caroled with some of the other faculty members on campus. This year she'd hoped to participate, but grading last-minute essays had kept her away once again. Next year she'd plan her time better so she could get involved again.

Determined not to allow anything to dampen her mood, she left her rocker, washed her bowl, and set up her laptop. Soft clicking from her keyboard was all the caroling she needed.

## *Chapter Two*

Margaret stared at the computer screen. Nothing. She slumped back in her chair, and for the umpteenth time reread the paragraphs she'd written. She frowned. The words were lifeless, dull, meaningless.

She hit the delete button. Again.

Having had a story floating around in her head for weeks, she couldn't wait to have the peace and quiet of the cabin to get her ideas into the computer, but, tonight the words weren't coming.

Disappointment settled around her. How could she think about writing fiction when her real life was in such turmoil? Ever since receiving the call from one of her old colleagues with a job offer, she'd had to think about her future. Everyone else said the job on the West Coast was made in heaven. More money. A prestigious title. Time to do research.

On paper it did sound perfect. So why wasn't she happy?

Pulling her gaze away from the blank screen, she exhaled loudly. *I have the position if I want it, so what's wrong with me?*

The pressure of deciding had exhausted her beyond thinking. She closed the program, stopped thinking about the job offer, and called it a night.

The crackle of the fire and the night sounds of the forest relaxed her as soon as she curled onto her side in the bed. Snuggled under a heavy patchwork quilt, she let herself be lulled to sleep.

But it didn't last.

The clock on the mantel had told her it was a little after two when she first opened her eyes. Now it was nearly four-thirty and she still lay awake. At first she reveled in the idea of lying awake, not having to worry about getting up fresh to face the responsibilities of running a department or being prepared for her English classes.

Now she was bored. Several times she'd gotten up to stoke the fire. She'd even sat with her feet curled in the rocker and watched while one of the new logs sizzled, then finally glowed into a nice flame.

Closing her eyes, she imagined a time not too long

ago when she'd lain in this same bed with a book while Edward sat in the rocker and read. She tried to remember how it felt to run her fingers through his gray hair. It wasn't often that he'd laugh out loud, but that motion always produced an embarrassed chuckle.

She smiled at the memory because recently it was getting harder and harder to visualize specifics about Edward. That bothered her. Bothered her a lot. Tonight she was glad he was with her even if it was only in thought.

To ward away the loneliness of the night, she curled into a tight ball and peeked once again at the fire. This time instead of seeing Edward sitting in his rocker, Paul Reynor in his plaid jacket knelt by the woodbin.

She blinked. "Where did that come from?"

Her spoken words sliced through the quiet of the night and startled her almost as much as the vision of the man by her fireplace. Guilt washed over her like the waterfall that flowed endlessly a short distance from her cabin. How could she even think about a perfect stranger when her heart and her mind were on Edward?

Punching the pillow into shape, she groaned out loud and waited for sleep to come. She thought she'd dozed off, but as five o'clock stared at her, she threw the blankets off and decided to start her day.

Mornings were her most productive hours to write. With her cup of coffee beside her and a huge fire raging in the background, she flipped open her laptop. This time she had completed three pages before the sun peeked over the tall pine trees.

"Now, that's more like it."

Satisfied with her work, she headed out for a brisk walk over a trail of fresh snow. She walked far enough toward the waterfall to hear its roar, but going all the way would require a lot more time than she was willing to give today. She stood quietly and pictured the roaring white water. That was enough for now. She felt invigorated and eager to return to her cabin to spend the rest of the day writing.

By three o'clock she had accomplished all she'd wanted to do. Turning off the computer, she smiled with contentment, then grabbed her coat for another walk before supper. While she had buried herself behind her computer screen, more snow had fallen making the scene clean and pristine.

"This is wonderful," she said out loud as she walked down the path, marveling at her fresh footsteps. Breathing the clear air, she slowed her pace to examine several tracks of deer and watched a thrush dart under a pile of brush.

She stooped down close to the snow. *Are there sights like this on the West Coast? Do I give all this up for a more prestigious title?* She'd gone all day without worrying about the offer. Why'd she have to think about it now?

Brushing the snow from her coat, she headed out along the trail once more. Before long she stepped into an opening directly across from the park's main office. Several vehicles sat in front of the log cabin, but Paul's old truck was not among them. He'd told her that he'd be back on Monday, but not seeing his truck sent a shock of disappointment through her.

Immediately she pulled up memories of when she and Edward walked these trails together. She closed her eyes and tried to remember what he looked like in his neck scarf, long wool coat, and tweed hat. She smiled. Today she had no trouble seeing him.

"That's better," she said and scared away another thrush.

Edward had never been a big talker, just walked along the paths in silence, periodically pointing out something of interest. Especially in the last couple of years of their marriage, Edward had said very little. He'd become a quiet, distinguished gentleman, always reading or studying.

Margaret remembered how she'd been so impressed with all his knowledge when they'd first married. She still had been after eight years of marriage, but now she remembered how, as the years went by, she sometimes wished he'd talk more or they'd socialized a little more than they did.

Not liking where her daydream was taking her, she stooped down and watched the thrush come out of hiding then ignore her as he busied himself with finding food. She thought how Paul must enjoy the birds in the park.

She blinked, frowned, then stood up. *Why'd I think of Mr. Reynor again? He's been kind to me. That's all. That's the only reason he's creeping into my thoughts. Again.*

Looking back to the office, she wondered if she dared to drop in on Joe and some of the other office personnel. She knew Joe would welcome her with open arms.

It was tempting, but convincing herself she hadn't come to the mountains to socialize with the guys in the office, she turned back toward the cabin rather than tramping down the snow-covered trail.

"Mrs. Daniels, is that you?"

Margaret bolted around at the sound of her name. Joe and Paul stepped from the tree line with shovels in their hands.

Margaret's hand flew to her chest. "Joe. Mr. Reynor. You startled me."

Joe stepped into the road and brushed snow from his sleeve. "We didn't mean to scare you, Mrs. Daniels."

"That's okay," she said as she sucked in a loud breath. "I guess I was deep in thought. The scenery here is just so beautiful. I never get my fill of it." Feeling a bit flustered because she'd been caught standing alone in the middle of the road staring at the office, she coughed and stuck her hands in her pocket.

Paul leaned on his shovel handle. He didn't look flustered at all with the afternoon light sparkling in his eyes. "Did that fire ever get going for you yesterday?"

She nodded. "It's wonderful. Thank you again for the wood."

He shrugged. "Not a biggy."

Joe put his hands on his hips and leaned back to stretch his back muscles. "It's a good thing he's here or you'd be hauling that wood for yourself. My arthritis is doing a number on me this winter."

"I'm so sorry, Joe. Let me know if I can do anything for you."

She looked at Paul and tried to ignore the tingle that radiated through her body just standing by this man. "I hadn't expected to see anyone out here in the woods, especially you. I didn't see your truck. I thought you wouldn't be back until tomorrow."

Paul chuckled. "My brother-in-law got called back into work last night so the whole family packed up and left my house. I saw no reason to sit alone when Joe could use me here. That old truck is one all of us use around here. One of the other guys is using it now. That black truck parked off to the side is mine."

Margaret glanced back at the office and nodded as

she saw a new extended cab. "Looks a little more reliable than that other one."

They all laughed at that, but it was Joe who spoke up. "Yeah, but that old truck has gotten me out of some sticky situations. She's been a good one." He rubbed his shoulder. "A little better than this shoulder's been this year, but you complain loud enough about your aches and pains, and the young kids finally listen and help out a little more." He glanced over at Paul.

Paul laughed. "Kid, huh? That's a new one. I haven't been called a kid for over two decades, but I'll take that as a compliment."

Joe straightened his thin shoulders. "Oh, it's a compliment, all right. When you get as old as I am, it's even hard to remember the last time someone used the word *kid* around you."

The warm exchange between the two men lightened Margaret's mood. "I hope when I'm your age, I'm still kicking like you are."

"I don't know about kicking, but I'm still moving, slow, but steady." He laughed, took a step into the road, then threw a quick look back to her. "Paul put a roast in the oven before we left. He doesn't look like he'd know his way around the kitchen, but the big guy never fails to surprise me. Why don't you join us? You won't be sorry."

The invitation to eat at the main office caught her off guard. Joe had never invited her before, and now that he had, she didn't know what to say.

From the corner of her eye she saw Paul straighten up. Was he uncomfortable with the compliment or the possibility he might have to share an evening with her?

"Come on, Mrs. Daniels. It's just Paul and me. We'd love the company. I like the man, but eating with him every night when he's here gets old."

Having Paul deliver wood to her cabin then offering him a cup of chocolate was totally different from spending an evening in a tiny kitchen. "I don't know, Joe. I really ought to get back to my computer."

Joe slapped his leg. "That's the lamest excuse I've ever heard. What do you think, Paul?"

He shrugged as if he understood how she felt. Maybe he felt the same way. Was Joe trying to play matchmaker?

"It's up to the lady of course, but I for one would like some company other than you." Paul speared her with a look that said he really did understand if she refused.

Joe didn't let the subject drop. "I've seen what you haul into that cabin and live on for two or three weeks. You can't eat just cans of soup for the time you're here."

"Okay," Margaret finally agreed. "You've convinced me. I was going to have chicken noodle tonight, but it can wait."

Paul watched Mrs. Margaret Daniels trudge through the snow-covered slope that led to the main office. Over her tall, thin frame she wore a long camel-colored coat that looked like something he'd seen on the mannequins in Paris. He admired nice clothes, and at one time placed a much higher value on their importance than he did today. Now the few nice pieces he still owned were squeezed in the back of his closet draped in plastic waiting to be worn for weddings or funerals.

Paul ran his hand down the front of his plaid jacket and smiled. Didn't quite match the elegance of Margaret's wool coat, but it was all he needed. Jeans, thick insulated shirts, and heavy boots were now his daily attire. That suited him just fine.

Walking a couple of steps behind them, Paul kept his eye on Margaret. She walked with the grace of a dancer, her steps light and fluid. As he picked his way down the slope, he could almost imagine holding her in his arms, twirling and floating across a dance floor. She would be liquid in his arms as she followed his lead and leaned into his body.

Joe turned around pulling him out of his daydream. "You back there, Paul?"

Feeling silly to have been thinking such thoughts,

he coughed then answered. “Oh yeah. Bringing up the rear. Somebody’s gotta do it.”

He heard Joe laugh, then he chuckled along with him, though for a different reason. How had he allowed himself to think about dancing or doing anything social with this elegant lady? As far as she was concerned, he was nothing more than a manual laborer in a low-paying job at a state park. That was okay with him. He liked what he did now and the last thing he needed was to dream about some sophisticated teacher from an elite college.

“Yep, somebody’s gotta bring up the rear and this evening, that’s me.”

Margaret and Joe both looked back at him, but it was Margaret’s broad smile that nearly took his breath away. The few remaining rays of the afternoon sun fighting their way through the snow clouds reflected off her perfectly lined teeth and highlighted the high cheekbones and big brown eyes.

To him she was beautiful, but not with a kind of beauty that would dazzle a crowd of people. Instead, it was subtle and quiet, probably the way she was.

He liked that. Again, he pushed that thought from his mind. It didn’t matter what he liked about her. She was a guest at a park where he worked, nothing more, and it was his job to make her feel comfortable and safe. He’d have to keep reminding himself of that, no matter how much he thought he might like to get to know her a little better.

As the three of them stepped into the office, the pungent smells of a roast and vegetables surrounded them.

Margaret pulled off her coat and hung it on a coat rack. "Oh, my, this smells wonderful. Much, much better than my chicken noodle soup ever could. I'm so glad you convinced me to come."

"I'm sure you won't be disappointed." Joe walked toward the corner of the office where a small partition separated the tiny space used for a kitchen, filled a glass with water, then turned back toward them.

"Make yourself at home, Mrs. Daniels. Paul will show you where everything is. I'm going to lie down a bit before supper." Joe then disappeared into the bedroom area.

Paul hung his coat on a rack. "I worry about old Joe this winter. He's having a hard time with this cold."

"I've noticed, but he still works every day. You have to admire him for that." She looked over at the kitchen area. "Can I help you finish our meal?"

"I'd like that." From the refrigerator he pulled out an assortment of vegetables. "Want to throw together a salad?"

"That's my specialty."

Not wasting any time, Margaret took the vegetables straight to the sink and began washing them. Paul set the tiny table by himself, all the time glancing in Margaret's direction to see if she needed help. At least that's what he told himself. He had to admit he liked watching her in the kitchen. She looked at home even surrounded by simple appliances jammed into a nook.

He remembered what she'd said about selling her home and wondered what it had looked like. He could picture her standing on stone floors and working on tiled countertops with elaborate cabinets and modern appliances.

But then he nearly chuckled out loud. She probably had a housekeeper who cooked for her and her husband. He couldn't image her scrubbing bathrooms or washing down walls, and she certainly didn't look like the domestic type to whip up a pot of stew or warm up leftovers from the night before. When she cooked, it was probably gourmet recipes with fancy ingredients and served in tiny portions.

Of course, she sounded perfectly content to be eating her can of soup and looked right at home in Joe's tiny kitchenette.

No, this lady professor wasn't his type at all, not that he was looking for a housekeeper or a cook. Those could be hired. He wasn't sure what he was looking for or if he was looking at all. He just knew Margaret was much too similar to his ex-fiancée Lydia to let his interest continue.

*Been there. Done that.*

But even as those thoughts formed, he had a feeling he'd have a hard time convincing himself to pretend she was just another guest at the park. And outwardly, she might have the sophistication that Lydia worked so hard to have, but he had a feeling that Margaret was different.

She placed a small bowl of salad in the middle of the table. "If you'll show me where you keep the knives, I'll help carve your roast." Her words cut into his daydream.

Paul positioned the paper napkin on the table and winked at her. "Just happen to know where you might find such a thing. We can work on the roast together."

He pulled open a drawer separated from the rest of the kitchen drawers and found a knife he thought she might be able to use. "We ran out of space and decided to take advantage of this counter over here. Isn't real convenient when you're cooking, but it works."

She shrugged. "If it works, it's perfect."

He lifted the roaster from the oven, found a serving platter, then carved the meat while she arranged the vegetables around the slices. The close domestic scene surprised him and touched him deeply. Every so often he was reminded how he'd missed out on this part of life.

Not wanting to dampen the homey mood, he finally straightened up and smiled. "Hey, now that platter looks pretty good if you ask me."

At that moment Joe stepped out of the bedroom area with the distinct smell of analgesic cream on his body. "Is it ready?"

"Sure is," Margaret said, not mentioning the fact that he reeked of medicinal odors.

Paul hadn't missed the tiny wrinkle in her nose when Joe had first stepped into the office area, but she was too much of a lady to say anything about the odor. He snickered to himself. "What do you say, Joe? You ready to try this roast I put on?"

Joe hobbled over to the table and took a seat. "Oh yeah. This is nice. Got two people to wait on me tonight."

Paul carried the tray over to the table while Margaret filled glasses with warm cider. "Don't get any ideas," he said to Joe. "We'll wait on you tonight. Might even do the dishes for you, but that complaining you did out there isn't going to get it with me."

Ignoring Paul, Joe grunted and motioned for him to sit. "Let's get this show on the road. I'm starving." He grabbed Margaret's hand and bowed his head at the same time that Paul took her other one into his.

With a faint smile on her lips, she bowed her head but hardly heard the rapid words that Joe mumbled.

At his quick "Amen" she slid her hand from Paul's and let out the long breath she'd been holding.

Margaret quickly served Joe's plate with thick slices of roast, pieces of cut potatoes and slices of carrots. It reminded her of serving Edward, but then she looked up at Joe and realized that Joe was an old man.

Her breath caught in her throat. Had Edward looked like that?

She shook her head. Edward had been about twenty years older than she was. At twenty-four, she thought he was the most handsome man she'd ever seen. When he proclaimed his love for her, she didn't hesitate to accept his proposal. Maybe he was starting to show his age then. Maybe he knew he wouldn't live long and couldn't waste any more time. Whatever it was, they had a quiet wedding and a quiet eight years together.

She looked at Joe again. He wasn't much older than Edward had been. Had she seen Edward through the eyes of a young, infatuated instructor all the years they'd been together?

"Mrs. Daniels?"

Margaret jerked her head up and looked at Paul.

"You must've been in deep thought. Sorry, I didn't mean to startle you."

Pulling her thoughts back into the ranger station,

she tried to smile. "I'm sorry. I guess I was thinking about all the work I'd done today. I really was productive."

Paul reached for a piece of bread, spread butter across it, then looked up at her. "Joe said you do some writing. That's interesting."

Margaret was fascinated by the softness of his eyes against the rugged lines of his face. To keep from staring, she reached for her drink before answering him.

"Yes, I write, but I do it only as an outlet. I'm not a serious author. I've been published in several English journals, but that's not a big deal. All of us on the faculty are expected to submit."

She took a sip of her drink. Surprised that he seemed interested in her pastime, she continued. "I'm not published in fiction, and it's fiction that I like to play with when the time permits. That's one of the reasons I enjoy coming up here. I have time to myself."

"Fiction, huh? Romance?" Paul asked with a twinkle in his eye.

His look sent a tiny thrill down her spine, but she stifled her emotion and answered in a calm voice. "Yes, I'm sure it's something you'd never read." She sipped her warm cider again. "It's fun and it's an escape even for the writer."

Paul cut a small piece of roast and lifted it with his

fork, but before he took a bite, he looked up at her. "We all need an escape."

"And what do you do as an escape?" All of a sudden she wanted to know what this man did beyond the park's boundaries.

She watched him think about her question as he took another bite, then a sip of his cider. From the hint of a smile curling his lips before he answered her, she knew that whatever he was thinking gave him a great deal of pleasure.

"I do carpentry," he finally said. "In a way, I guess that's an escape."

"Carpentry? That's interesting and, if you think about it, that's similar to what I do."

"No, I don't think so," he said.

"Sure it is," she continued. "You build with wood and I build with words. In the end we've both produced something that earlier had only been visible to our minds."

He pinned her with his brown eyes. Finally he nodded. "Okay, I'll agree, but I guess I never looked at it that way before."

Joe looked up from his plate. "The man can build anything he sets his mind to. He's a genius. You'll need to take her to see your work someday, Paul."

Not even sure what he built, where it was, or what it entailed, she still answered enthusiastically. "Yes, I'd like that very much."

Paul looked from Joe to her. “Maybe before you leave the park we can take a ride down into the valley and I’ll show you how I spend my time. I have to warn you, Joe might be exaggerating a bit when he says I’m a genius.”

“I’ll have to be the judge of that. It’s a deal. I’d love to see your work.” She stuck out her hand and they shook on it before she changed her mind.

## *Chapter Three*

For three days after Joe and Paul shared their meal with her, Margaret kept to herself. Paul was glad. As much as he wanted to see her again, he knew the needy feelings that disturbed his days and invaded his dreams came with the long winter nights and the approaching holidays, not from the fact that he and Margaret had anything in common.

Paul put away the last of the dishes that he and Joe had used for their evening meal. Paul had started hanging around longer with Joe, who now sat in his rocker asleep. Winter was playing havoc with the older man this year and Paul hated to leave him alone for too long.

Taking the dishcloth, he wiped down the countertop, rinsed the sink, then polished the stainless steel with a dry cloth.

As he was pulling on his coat to head back into town, the telephone rang. He grabbed it and listened while someone asked if he could get a message to Dr. Daniels.

Quickly, he ran through the mental list of the few guests at the park. "Uh, I don't think we have a Dr. Daniels listed in any of the cabins, but . . ."

Joe raised his head. "That's Margaret. She's Dr. Daniels."

Paul stared at Joe, knowing his look of surprise must be evident, then turned his attention back to the telephone. "Uh, sorry, sir. Someone just told me who that is. I'll be glad to get a message to her. Let me grab something to write with."

He dug through a drawer, the entire time thinking about Margaret being *Dr.* Daniels. He wasn't surprised.

"Okay, shoot. What's the message?"

He wrote while the man on the other end talked, read the message back to him, then assured him he'd get it to her tonight. When he hung up he looked over at Joe. "Dr. Daniels?"

Joe shrugged. "Yeah, but no one calls her that out here. The only way I knew she was a doctor was hearing Mr. Daniels call her that when he was pretending to be mad at her."

He let that thought sink in for a moment trying to visualize what a Mr. Daniels would look like. Nothing. "I wonder if he was a doctor as well."

"For some reason I think he was. Maybe she called him that one day."

Paul stood unmoving, thinking about this new development.

"What's the matter? Just because now you know she has a doctorate in some subject she teaches doesn't make her any different than she was ten minutes ago. She was sweet Margaret Daniels then and she's still sweet Margaret Daniels now."

"Hey, you know I admire people with education."

"Even women with higher degrees than yours?"

"Look, the woman is brilliant. Why wouldn't she have a doctorate?"

"So what's the problem?"

"No problem, except you're sticking your nose into something that doesn't concern you."

"Does she know about your background?"

"There you go again. That nose is going to get you in deep trouble." He plopped a cap on his head and grabbed the message. "I'll drop this off on my way out. Are you going to sleep now or can I tell her she can come up to use your phone?"

"I guess I'll stay up a few more minutes for her." Joe pretended to grumble, but Paul knew the old man looked forward to Margaret's visits.

Paul wasn't sure, but he thought he heard Joe say something about a dumb engineer as he headed out to his truck.

He and Margaret hadn't talked much about what she did at the college. He'd gathered she taught English from their meager conversation, but he had no idea she had such a respected title. He was impressed, but he couldn't ignore the response that he couldn't control—having a prestigious position as she did meant she was deeply imbedded in a social life that he'd long since given up.

He pulled up in front of her cabin, where only one small light shone behind the curtain. He hoped she'd heard the truck drive up. He didn't want to alarm her, but even as those thoughts were forming in his head, the front porch light came on and Margaret opened the door.

She stood in the door dressed in soft pink lounging clothes that contrasted with her dark hair hanging loose around her face. Even in silhouette, she looked much too young to be a boring professor and a widow to boot.

Paul knew the moment she recognized him. She opened the door wider and smiled. "Good evening, Mr. Reynor. What brings you out to my little neck of the woods?"

The crunch of the ice beneath his feet drowned out his low chuckle. *Do I look that old to her?*

"Mr. Reynor's my father. My name's Paul, remember?"

"Okay, Paul, what brings you out here?"

As Paul stepped up on the stoop near her, a soft hint of strawberries touched his nose. At a closer look, he realized her hair was still a little wet and her skin shone fresh and clean without a touch of make-up. "I have a message for you. Hope you don't mind the intrusion. I can see you were getting ready for a quiet night."

"Oh, no. Quiet is nice, but a friendly visitor is much, much better. Please come in."

Together they stepped inside. Paul swallowed when he caught the glow of the fire reflecting softly against her skin. He reeled in the urge to reach out and touch her face.

"You say I have a message?"

"Yes, ma'am." He handed her the name and number on a slip of paper. "The man said he'd be at that number for about the next hour then you could probably catch him on his cell. That's the bottom number."

She glanced at the name and sighed.

"Trouble?"

"No. Just the dean of our college. I'm sure it's just something that needs to be clarified with a grade. Who knows. I can't imagine it being anything more serious than that."

"I'll be glad to take you up to the office."

"Oh, no. I can drive up there."

Paul shuffled his feet. "I know you can drive, but I'm asking if I can drive you up. It's starting to snow and it's dark. I'd feel better if you'd let me take you."

Margaret looked hesitant to accept his offer.

"Look. I'm not in any hurry to get home tonight. I'd like to know you are safe and sound back in your cabin before I pulled out of the park. Call it my sworn duty to our park guests."

Her face softened into a smile. "Well, if you put it that way. I'd hate for you to be slack on your duties."

She pulled her coat off the hook on the wall. As she reached around to put her arm into the sleeve, Paul reached out and lifted it to her body. For a second, she froze, then looked up into his eyes and smiled. "Thank you. I haven't had a lot of help these past few years. It still stuns me when someone offers."

"Well, the men on your campus must be living in the dark ages if they don't rush to assist a beautiful woman like you." He almost bit his tongue for voicing the compliment, but when she laughed, he felt better knowing he hadn't made her uncomfortable.

She slipped on leather gloves and a scarf. "Let's go so I can see which student is complaining about his C."

He couldn't keep his chuckle from escaping as they stepped outside the cabin. "C's are good, especially in English, if I remember right."

When he slid in behind the wheel, she picked up their conversation. "And I guess you were a C student in English classes, huh?"

"Yep, and proud to get them." He laughed. "Math and science were my subjects. Loved trig and geometry. Guess that's why I went into construction." He stopped there, not wanting to talk about his engineering background with the government. "I kind of liked history as well."

Even in the dark of the truck, Paul could see the excitement in her eyes when she answered. "I like history too. I teach literature, and I spend as much time with the history of the literary periods as with the literary works. You can't separate them. The literature depends on the lifestyle."

"Yeah, I guess it does. Hadn't thought much about it." For that matter he hadn't thought about literature classes in a very long time, but listening to Margaret talk, he wished he could've had an English teacher with her enthusiasm and outward love of the subject. Maybe he would've pulled more than a C.

He smothered another chuckle thinking about his college days as they pulled up to the cabin.

Margaret reached for the door handle. "I won't be

but a minute. You don't have to come in unless, of course, you want to."

"Nope. I'll be glad to wait right here and keep the truck warm. Tell Joe I'll see him bright and early tomorrow."

He watched her walk into the office and wondered what her conversation would be about. What he really wanted to do was to stand by her and eavesdrop, but since he had no reason to go in, he figured he'd better stay put in the truck.

Just as she predicted, she wasn't inside more than five minutes. When she opened the cabin door, Joe stepped out with her and Paul smiled as the old man gave her a fatherly kiss on the cheek.

"Well, just as I figured," she said as she climbed back into the truck. "Two students are already complaining about their grades."

"And?"

"And nothing. I'll check to make sure my math is correct, but that's the only reason I'd change a grade. I don't give grades lightly. I slave over each one before actually recording it. Nope. The grades stick unless I made a mathematical mistake."

"You mean your boss called you during your vacation to tell you that?"

She fidgeted in her seat. "He really called to invite me to his home on Friday. He's having some of the department heads over for a holiday drink and he wanted me to come in to meet a new lady who'll be joining us on the first of the year."

Paul took his eyes off the road and looked at her. "Don't tell me you're the head of your department. You're too young."

"That's sweet of you to say such a thing, but, yep, I'm the head of the English Department."

He whistled. "I'm impressed, but tell me, now that I know you've got a PhD and you're the head of the department, should I call you Dr. Daniels?"

Looking embarrassed, she rolled her eyes. "First, don't be impressed. I was lucky enough to get my degrees younger than most. Second, some of our older professors retired and the younger ones left for bigger schools. That left me." She shrugged. "Not a big deal, really. It just means I have a lot of extra work to do. And for your other question, that's a definite no. I come up here to get away from all that."

He really was impressed with her accomplishments, but her being the head of the department put her up one more step on the social ladder, a ladder he didn't want to touch with a ten-foot pole.

He knew what that ladder was all about. Getting burned one time by a woman like that was all it took to teach him a lesson. He'd had enough of that high-society stuff with Lydia. All she'd wanted from him was his money. Without the high-paying government contracts, he was nothing in her eyes.

*Nope. Don't need that again.*

She pulled him out of his reverie. "I can't believe Dr. Sabastian called me Dr. Daniels when he asked for me. Don't you dare use that title out here. I'm Margaret. Period."

He smiled. "Okay, Margaret Period, so are you going to the party?"

She rolled her head back against the seat. "I think I have no choice. Dr. Sabastian has never before called me during my break, so it must be something that he feels strongly about. I always carry a nice outfit in case something like this comes up, but I'm not real excited about having to go." She grimaced.

"It's one of those gotta-do-it-for-my-career parties, huh?"

"I guess, but don't get me wrong. I love the Sabastians. They've been like parents to me, especially since Edward's death. He and Dr. Sabastian were very good friends, and after the funeral, they took me under their wings. So, to answer your question, yes, it's one of those job parties, but underneath, it's much more."

"They sound like wonderful people."

Her beautiful smile told him she agreed.

Even though he knew he needed to stay clear of another woman like Lydia, Paul fought the urge to tell her he'd drive her to the social then bring her back to the park, but he kept his thoughts to himself. He didn't know her well enough to step into her business.

*Thank goodness.*

But even as his mind told him that not offering was the right thing to do, his body wasn't cooperating.

She turned around and smiled at him as they pulled up to her cabin. "Would you like to come in for that cup of chocolate that I never got to fix for you?"

"It's tempting, but it's also late." No way would he go into her cabin alone with her this evening, not with his emotions knocking around in his chest. He wasn't sure what was going on with himself, but he had more sense than to tempt fate.

"I need to get home. Looks like the snow's starting to come down again, and I'd rather not drive in it if I don't have to. I'll take a rain check on that chocolate though."

He could've sworn that a wave of disappointment swept across her face, but she instantly gained her composure, sat up straight, then opened the door. "Thanks so much for delivering the message. We'll drink that hot chocolate some other time."

When she looked back at him, he had the distinct urge to lean into her body to kiss her. Her lips were full and inviting, and he would have given anything to feel their softness against his own. But it was her eyes that took his breath. There was a sadness in them he wanted to take away. Blinking, he pushed that thought aside. Delivering a message was one thing. Kissing a park guest was another.

Instead of leaning toward her, he straightened himself against the door and nodded. "Take care."

Margaret waited on the stoop as Paul drove away, then stood alone even as his taillights disappeared through the trees. She pulled her coat tighter across her chest. All of a sudden the thought of going into the empty cabin didn't appeal, but then as she let her gaze move around the dark forest, she let out a tiny chuckle. "Can't stay out here either."

Closing the door behind her and making sure the lock was in position, she looked around determined to find something productive to do. She'd been sitting at the desk trying to write before Paul had driven up. She walked over to the laptop, turned it on, and clicked on her current project file. One pitiful paragraph had been added before the crunch of Paul's tires gave her blood a little jumpstart.

How long would she have sat there staring at the screen had he not come? Without having to put a lot of thought into it, she pointed the arrow to Exit and shut down the computer. She wasn't ready to stare at the screen again.

She found the classical radio station that had

always filled the cabin with music on evenings when she and Edward had sat together quietly and rocked. After a few songs she frowned and hit the Seek button. Finding a soft-rock station, she settled back in her rocker and tried to remember why she enjoyed sitting up here in the mountains alone.

## *Chapter Four*

Friday finally arrived. Usually Margaret hated leaving the park during her holiday, but this year she was glad to have something to do. In a way she actually looked forward to getting away and socializing with some of her faculty associates.

Never before had she been bored with her days at the cabin, but this year something was missing. Or, if she were honest with herself, something or someone had been added that made her look at herself and her time at the cabin a little closer.

Her nerves had been strung taut when she'd left campus. Now that she'd had time to relax, her nerves were better, her body was rested, but her emotions were jumbled.

She wasn't sure what she needed to do. At least

the social at Dr. Sabastian's house would give her a distraction from her boredom and from a certain man down at the ranger's station.

Paul had done nothing but show kindness to a woman alone in the park, but in doing so he had touched something deep within her. He had been gracious and friendly and helpful, nothing more. So why was she experiencing emotions she'd hidden years ago?

Living with Edward had been comfortable, not exciting, just comfortable. When he'd died, Margaret Olivia Daniels, had to face the world again alone. For all her education, social training, and career achievements, it had scared her to death. Underneath all the degrees and titles that followed her name lay the mousey-haired, gawky girl who'd never gone out on a date until Dr. Edward Daniels took her under his wing and fell in love with her.

Letting her mind enjoy that thought only for a second, she brushed her hair back into a severe coiffure and inserted a black onyx hairpin. Before removing her fingers, she ran them down its shiny length. It had been a gift from Edward on their second anniversary.

*Enough of that.* She stepped back from the mirror. Turning to the side and straightening her shoulders, she took a long look at herself. She knew she had gained a lot more grace over the years, but she was still willowy and lacked the necessary curves that made a woman attractive to a man.

She sighed. A man like Paul Reynor would want a voluptuous woman with strength and stamina to keep up with him. She'd have to be fun to take out to a local tavern, sit around a table with friends, share a bottle of beer with, and dance into the wee hours of the night.

She didn't know how to do those things. She never had the opportunity to try.

She humphed. *A lot of good three degrees in English does me. Who'd want to talk about Tennyson sitting around a bar?*

Pulling the black silk dress off its hanger, she slipped it over her head. It wasn't a new dress, but it still draped nicely against her body and it was something she could wear to many different functions. Examining herself once more in the mirror, she was satisfied that it was a good outfit for the cocktail party tonight. She decided to wear her fur-lined boots in the car and simply carry her black strapped heels until she arrived at the Sabastians.

With a dab of lipstick, she was ready to go.

Putting a few necessities into a simple evening bag, she took her coat from the hanger and headed out the door. No new snow had fallen today so she felt comfortable about driving through the park and down into the valley. Except for the extremely cold temperatures that had descended on the area over night, the evening was perfect.

That is until she turned the key in the ignition. At first she heard a foreign-sounding grind, then nothing. Keeping her cool, she sat behind the wheel and let the engine demons wake up and do what they were supposed to do.

Again, she turned the key. Nothing.

"Well, phooey," she said out loud. "Now what?" She couldn't believe this was happening. Not today. Not when she'd gotten herself up for the gathering. She tried the key in the ignition again and again, but nothing worked. Finally she hit both hands on the steering wheel in frustration and flopped back against the seat.

In her mind she started calculating how much it would cost for a taxi to come out to the park to take her into town. That was silly. Even if she could get someone to come up here, it would cost an arm and a leg. Then she thought maybe she could offer to pay Paul to take her.

"Bad idea." Again the words floated around the cold interior of the car. She shivered.

Deciding to figure it out in the warmth of the cabin, she opened the door, but stopped as she saw Paul's black truck coming down the trail. A tingle crept up her spine and a smile curled her lips.

She stayed in the car and watched as he pulled his

truck alongside her town car. Frowning, he hopped out of the truck.

"Something wrong, Margaret?"

She motioned for him to get in the car. When he'd slid his big frame onto the front seat, he looked at her and shook his head. "Dead battery?"

"Dead something. I guess it's the battery. I didn't realize it was supposed to get as cold as it did last night. I guess I should have done something to protect it."

Rubbing his hand across his chin, he frowned. "I started to come up here to remind you to protect the car, but I was called out on several other problems and left the park late." He shook his head. "Sorry."

"Hey, it's not your fault that I forgot how cold it gets up here."

"I've got some jumper cables, but I have to tell you, sometimes they don't work when the car's been sitting out for this long."

"I'd appreciate it if you'd try though."

He started to get out, then turned back around. "You on your way to the campus party?"

She nodded.

"Well, don't worry. You look too pretty to sit out here in the woods. We'll make sure you get there."

At that he got out of the car. Even sitting in her cold vehicle, his simple words and his take-control presence warmed her as no fireplace could.

He'd said she was pretty. Edward used to tell her that as well. She knew she wasn't beautiful, but she also knew that over the years she'd learned to work with what God had given her and to fill in the gap at cosmetic counters, classy dress shops, and beauty salons. It had been exciting to find the crack and step out of her shell of shyness.

She might have been a quiet intellectual when Edward married her, but she soon found the enjoyment of socializing with members of their college friends.

Beautiful? No. But she now had the confidence to feel beautiful. Paul's words reminded her how sweet a compliment could be.

Hoping she wasn't being vain, she relaxed against the seat and watched Paul work on her dead engine. He tried using the jumper cables to charge her battery from his. He squirted something from a can onto the engine. She thought she heard him mumbling words into the engine and wondered it he was trying to sweet-talk it. That thought brought a smile to her face.

But, when he yanked the door open again and jumped in, she knew that the sweet talk hadn't worked.

"Pretty dead, huh?" she asked.

"Oh yeah. You killed it all right. Now, this is what we can do. I've got one other thing to do before I can leave the park, but if you'll wait in your cabin, I'll finish up, wash some of this grime off me, then I'll escort you right to the door of your dean's house. When the party's over, you can call me and I'll bring you right back up here if it hasn't started snowing again. If it has, we can each get a hotel room in town. If it's late and snowing, I'd rather not even venture back to my place."

As much as she'd like to take him up on her suggestion, Margaret shook her head. "Oh, no. I couldn't ask you to do that."

"Why not? Look, Margaret, this might be the weekend, but my calendar is about as empty as the life in that battery. Now get yourself inside before you get frostbite, and I'll be back in about thirty minutes. No arguments."

She opened her mouth to speak.

"No arguments, Dr. Daniels."

She did as she was told. After hanging her coat back on the hanger to wait for his return, she turned and caught a glimpse of herself in the mirror once more. This time the smile that was plastered across her face was hard to deny.

The ride down the mountain, through town, and then into the next one was filled with soft music from Paul's set of CDs. Margaret sat in comfortable silence most of the way, listening to him talk about the landmarks they were passing or make a comment about one of the songs on the radio.

Funny, she thought. Usually when she was thrust into a social situation with a man, her stomach knotted and her thoughts scattered as she tried to think of something sensible to say. This evening was different. She found she liked being in the truck with Paul. It felt as natural to her as standing at her podium in her classroom.

The sun set as they reached the bottom of the mountain. The interior of the truck was cozy and warm. Paul made it that way. Relaxed and casual, he sat on the driver's side, sometimes humming, sometimes not saying anything.

He was dressed in his usual red plaid jacket and jeans and acted as if driving someone to the house of the dean of a college was the most natural thing in the world for him to do. How did he do it? She admired anyone who had natural confidence, not the worked-at kind that she had. As long as she was in her environment on campus, she was in control. She could talk with anyone concerning a curriculum matter or a student matter. That was her life. This was not.

Paul stopped at a red light and turned to her. "You're awfully quiet this evening."

"Yes, I guess I am. I've been enjoying the ride

down the mountain. It's been a beautiful drive, and I was able to take it all in. I've been driving myself around for the past few years. You really miss a lot when you do that all the time."

He shrugged. "Hmm, I haven't thought about it that way. I drive all the time, but I guess you're right. Maybe I ought to let you drive back so I can take in the sights."

She giggled. Her eyes flew open. *Was that a giggle? Did I giggle like one of my students?*

This time he grinned. "You ought to do that more often."

At first she thought he was making fun of her, but when he looked at her with soft, caring eyes, she relaxed.

"You're very pretty when you smile," he added before she could answer. "You ought to let yourself smile more. Smiling's good for the soul."

His words hit bottom like concrete in a pool of water. Had she quit smiling? Did she ever smile enough? Certainly she had. She remembered getting her braces off at thirteen. She'd smiled so big for the first few days that her face hurt.

But she wasn't thirteen anymore. She turned her head and looked out the window. Had she gotten to be some morbid, depressing old woman at thirty-five?

"Margaret, I didn't mean to make you upset. I was

giving you a compliment. I'm sorry if I made you uncomfortable."

She turned back to him. "No. You didn't make me uncomfortable. I think you're probably right. I think I've gotten much too serious lately."

"Don't be too hard on yourself. Having to carry around a lot of responsibility has a way of making a person serious. I have a feeling your position puts a lot of demands on you."

"It does, but what you said is true. Smiling is good for the soul."

She let a grin spread across her face to cover the ache in her chest. "I think I'll write that down as one of my resolutions for this new year. Won't my students be surprised when I greet them with a smile to go with my morning lecture?"

## *Chapter Five*

Paul drove through town with the lights of campus shining through the trees. Margaret could envision the buildings of her small liberal arts college. The old brick buildings dating back to the eighteen hundreds gave Margaret a sense of place. It'd been that way from the first time she'd driven onto campus for her interview shortly after she'd finished her graduate studies and had a year of teaching under her belt.

It didn't take long to know that this campus was ideal for her. Even with the whirlwind of introductions and tours during that first week, she remembered feeling she belonged here. Her parents had sent her to one of the elite Ivy League schools and even though she'd appreciated their generosity, she didn't want to spend her entire teaching career there.

Hearing about the job opening at this college couldn't have come at a more perfect time for her. A straight-A average during undergraduate and graduate school helped her land what she considered the best position available in the country. Bigger colleges paid more, but that's not what she needed.

It was in those first few months on campus that she'd met Edward, and by the end of the first semester, she was Mrs. Edward Daniels. Her new campus met her needs. Her teaching position was ideal, and her marriage fit right into a comfortable situation.

Edward wasn't exciting, but neither had her life been before she met him. He loved her, and for that she was willing to give up the excitement of a romantic courtship. How can you miss something you've never had?

The memory of those first years with him warmed her.

Paul interrupted her reverie. "That smile tells me you're happy to be back home."

"Yes, I guess I am. After being here for so long, it is home even though I need to get away sometimes. I still like the feeling of coming back when I do return."

"Yeah. I get that feeling too."

"You live around here, you said?"

"I do, but where I live doesn't give me that feeling. It's where I'm going to live."

"And that is?"

He chuckled. "It's on the other side of the valley. I've been working on a house for a while. It's slow-going, but one day it'll be a place I can call home. Even now I feel that way and I don't live there yet."

"Well. You've gotten my interest piqued now. Will I get to see this place one day?"

"If you'd like. I love showing it off. We'll talk about it." He stopped at a stop sign. "Okay. Where to now?"

She pointed, then flipped down the lit mirror and applied another dab of lipstick. She then slipped her feet out of her boots and into her heels.

From the corner of her eye she saw that Paul glanced over at her as she changed shoes. She should have felt awkward, but she didn't.

He slowed down in front of an impressive home with massive columns and a wide front porch. "You sure you won't get too cold wearing just those shoes?"

"Probably, but I don't want to haul these boots in. Anyway, it's only a few steps up to the door since I have this wonderful escort service tonight."

Paul didn't hesitate. "When I pick you up, I'll meet you at the door with the boots so you can put them on before you come out. How's that?" He flashed her a smile that tickled her all the way to her toes.

"Now that's what I call service."

He gave her his cell phone number. "This doesn't work up in the park, but it does in town, so I'll be waiting."

"I feel like I've imposed so much on you already. I'll try not to stay late. As soon as I feel I've done my duty, I'll call you."

"Look, don't leave early because of me. I know the owner of a small café not far from here. I haven't visited in a long time so I'll enjoy having an excuse to sit and yak. You do what you have to do and don't worry about me. I'll call around to some hotels to see if there're any rooms available if we need to spend the night."

Margaret picked up her purse. As much as she had looked forward to getting out of the cabin tonight and coming here, now she would rather stay in the truck with Paul. Spending a quiet evening at a local café would suit her just fine. But of course, she couldn't. This gathering was part of her job.

Margaret rang the doorbell, but watched the black truck ease out of the driveway as she waited for the door to open. The man who'd hauled her firewood just four days ago had become a real person to her, someone whom she enjoyed being around.

"Come in, Dr. Daniels. Come in." Mrs. Sabastian greeted her as she reached out and took her hand. "I'm so glad you made it down the mountain."

Margaret pulled her attention away from the man with the twinkle in his eye and an ever-present smile on his lips. She became Dr. Margaret Daniels, English professor and head of the English Department, and extended her hand to greet her long-time friend and wife of the dean.

The evening gathering was pleasant. She met the lady who'd be teaching in her department and was delighted with her. She was young and vibrant, and Margaret knew the students would respond to her personality.

Warm eggnog and a beautifully-decorated table filled with holiday treats kept the guests happy. Margaret ate and drank and socialized, but all the while she wondered what Paul was doing at the café. She hoped he'd told the truth and really had someone to talk with for the evening.

Then a silly notion flitted through her brain. She wondered if that person was a female. Immediately she pushed that thought aside. What difference would it make? The man had offered her a ride to town. That's all. Paul was kind and generous and would have done the same for any of the other guests who found themselves stranded at his park.

Even so, she couldn't wait to hear how his evening had gone.

The dozen or so administrators and professors who came out to wish the Sabastians holiday cheer and to meet the new staff member melded well together. As the evening progressed, Margaret couldn't help but think of Edward. These people had been their social life during the eight years they'd been married.

Neither Edward nor she saw much of their family, so the faculty became their family, especially the Sabastians. Judith and Harold were so much more than a college dean and his wife. She loved them.

Edward had a brother living out West where they'd visited occasionally. Margaret thought about her own parents. Older than the parents of most of her classmates, they'd died peacefully within a year of the other shortly after she'd received her first degree. They'd lived a full life until the end, having the best of everything, including people to come in to take care of their house and yard and even a lady to care for their personal needs.

Her parents had been well-off and happy, but she didn't want to live their lifestyle. Their friends were part of the higher echelon of Boston society. As a young woman Margaret accepted her lifestyle, but couldn't wait to make a life of her own.

These people around her tonight became that life. She was grateful to them for helping her after Edward's death, but as she looked around, she knew that she couldn't limit her life to them. She had a lot in common with them, but could she spend the rest of her life with only this small circle of friends?

The application she'd filled out for a job at a West Coast university was supposed to take her away from the tiny campus and let her expand her horizons.

*But is that what I want?*

As if reading her mind from across the room, Harold stepped by her. "Have you heard from Dr. Hennings?"

"Yes, he called last week. Made me a nice offer."

"I see." He took a sip of brandy. "And what did you tell him?"

"I told him I'd think about it over the holidays."

"And have you?"

She laughed. "Why, certainly. It's a little hard not to think about the offer he made to me. You must have written him quite a letter of recommendation."

"It killed me, but I did. I knew he'd want you if I told the truth, but I had no choice. I guess we can't keep you sheltered here with us always."

Margaret thought about his words. They had sheltered her, but it was only because they had loved Edward so much and had come to feel the same about her.

Would she find people to care for her at a new campus?

Going up to the cabin this holiday season had given her the quiet-time she so wanted, but it had done more than that. Spending the little time that she had with Paul and with Joe had reminded her that there was life off campus and that there were people here who cared for her too.

Everyone kept telling her that she was still young and had to enjoy life. Maybe she'd do just that. But how? Was moving the way to do it?

The Mountain Ridge Café was nearly empty as Paul sat in a booth sipping coffee. He watched Barbara wipe down the counter once more while her husband, David, cleaned the kitchen. Paul knew David through his brother-in-law and stopped in to see them during the time he was trying to zero in on what he wanted to do with his life.

He'd already lived through the first phase of his life as he liked to call it. Those whirlwind, fast-paced, money-grabbing few years had taken him out of the country, stuffed his bank accounts, but nearly ruined the rest of his life. Those years had served him well, but he couldn't live like that forever.

Those years had shown him what he didn't want out of life and that was everything he'd had then, including the woman with whom he thought he'd spend the rest of his life.

*Funny how things work out,* he thought. Several years ago he'd felt as though his life had come to an end. After deciding that he had enough money, he sold his company to settle down in a small town with Lydia to enjoy life and raise a family. He had done what he'd set out to do, but now it was time to really tune in to living. Those plans didn't fit in with Lydia's at all.

Before he knew it, she had dumped him, and he was sitting here in this very booth, trying to figure out how he'd been so wrong about the woman he loved. But things did work out. One thing led to another, and when he rode up on the mountain with David to visit with Joe, he found what he'd been missing.

Barbara turned to him from behind the counter and dragged him out of his memories. "I have about one more cup of coffee left in this pot. Want it before I dump it?"

"Thanks, but if I drink any more coffee, I won't be able to sleep for a week."

She laughed, then started cleaning the big percolator. "If I box up a couple pieces of pie, will you take them with you? I know Joe would appreciate some."

"You know the answer to that. We love your pies. Got any more of that lemon? I'll pay for all you have left."

"Oh, phooey. You don't have to pay. I'm offering you what would probably be thrown away." She gathered up some take-out plates. "What time do you have to pick up that teacher friend of yours?"

Paul glanced down at his watch. "She ought to be calling soon. She didn't think she'd be late."

Barbara humphed.

"Okay, what's the problem? Spit it out if you have something to say."

"You know I don't like to stick my nose into other people's business."

He cut her off. "Now, don't start with a fib. You know you're in the middle of everyone's business in this end of town. I don't know why the newspaper bothers to waste their ink on stale news when they've got you."

"Paul Reynor, you know that's not true. I just happen to hear a lot of stuff working here. People tell me things whether I want them to or not."

He had a feeling he knew what she was about to say, but he'd let her voice the words anyway. "Okay, so what's on your mind?"

"Well, I don't know this lady-friend of yours."

"Her name's Dr. Daniels—Margaret Daniels—and she's a guest at the park."

"Yeah, yeah. I know all that." She snapped the top of several foam containers with the pie slices, then placed the pieces of the percolator in the sink before coming over to sit by Paul. The frown on her face told him he was in for a lecture. "I just wonder about people like that."

Paul reminded himself that Barbara was his friend, then swallowed his irritation. "People like what, Barbara?"

"People who spend their whole life buried on campuses like that. They don't socialize with the rest of the folks in town. You never see them unless you happen to run into one at the supermarket. I hear at some colleges they have their groceries delivered just so they don't have to ever leave. That's weird if you ask me."

Paul had heard stories like that, but not around here. It did make him wonder how often Margaret left campus.

"And," she continued, "what do you two have in common?"

At that Paul had to laugh. "I guess you might have a point there. She teaches English. In fact, she's the head of that department. What I remember about my literature classes can probably fit on this napkin, but so far she's been pretty easy to talk with. All those dead writers and poets haven't come up in our conversation yet."

He had to smile to himself. There hadn't been a time that Paul had been with Margaret when he hadn't enjoyed every second of their visit. Maybe enjoyed them too much.

Barbara humphed again. "Well, I hear all those

professors are stuck-up and think they're better than the rest of us in town."

Now Paul got on the defensive. "Don't start grouping people. Just because she lives on campus doesn't mean she's like that at all. I'll have to bring her in and let you meet her. I think you'd like her."

Barbara twisted the watch on her wrist. "Don't forget what Lydia did to you, Paul. David and I don't want to see you hurt again. Why don't you find you some nice girl from one of these farms around here and settle down?"

Paul laughed. "Thanks, Barbara. I'll remember your advice, but I'm just giving this lady a ride. Her battery died on her. I'm not trying to elope with her."

The cell phone sang as soon as he'd said that. He winked at Barbara before she slid out of the booth.

"You just remember all that." She straightened her broad shoulders and pulled the apron from around her neck. "I don't know if we have enough towels left to mop up after another failed courtship."

"Thank you, Barbara." He answered his cell phone eager to hear Margaret's voice, then tossed some money on the table as he slid out of the booth. "I'll remember your advice."

Paul did think about what Barbara had told him as he drove out to the campus to pick up Margaret. Barbara was right. At first glance he and Margaret had very little in common, but the more he got to know her the more he found that a warm person lived inside that proper exterior.

Pulling into the driveway as several cars pulled out, he wondered how she'd enjoyed herself. Was she a different person when she was with her colleagues? Was she shy and quiet as he'd observed at the park or was she outgoing and talkative in her own environment?

Wonder all he liked about the English professor Dr. Daniels, he'd probably never find out.

He stopped the truck, reached over for the boots, then walked up to the door. It opened before he had a chance to ring the bell. In the doorway stood a lady in her late fifties with gray-streaked brown hair and skin that still had a peaches-and-cream look about it. She was petite and the winter-white suit that she wore emphasized the fact that once she'd been a real beauty. Now she was simply elegant with a smile that radiated a friendly welcome.

"You must be Mr. Reynor? Come in. I'm Mrs. Sabastian. Dr. Daniels just walked to the back to speak with my husband, but she'll be back in a moment. She's been expecting you. Please come in out of the cold."

Paul extended his free hand. "Thank you. I will. I think the temperature's dropped ten degrees since I dropped Marga . . . uh, Dr. Daniels off."

He stepped into a cozy hall with several dark mahogany tables against the wall. With his appreciation of old furniture and fine workmanship, he could tell that what he saw in the house came from the best craftsmen. "This is a lovely home."

She beamed. "Why, thank you. It's been part of our lives since Harold started teaching here over fifteen years ago. I just love the place."

Immediately Paul liked the wife of this college dean. Mrs. Sabastian's smile looked genuine and her openness reminded him of his own mother.

Paul looked up as Margaret and a tall, older man stepped into the hall. His receding hairline and thick midsection couldn't hide the fact that he'd once been a formidable figure in his youth. Paul could see Dr. and Mrs. Sabastian as a young couple thirty years earlier, and a momentary longing for what they had swept across his chest. To find someone to share a lifetime would be the ultimate piece of happiness.

Of course, finding that someone wasn't easy, and it certainly wasn't worth risking a broken heart again.

Margaret smiled when she saw him. "Paul, I didn't know you'd arrived. I hope you haven't been waiting long. This is Dr. Sabastian."

"No, I just got here." He turned to Dr. Sabastian and shook the man's hand, exchanged cordial greetings and instantly decided he liked the man as well as his wife.

Dr. Sabastian stepped near his wife and draped an arm around her shoulder, unaware that the familiarity and love of that motion touched another string around Paul's heart.

"I'm glad to know someone is looking after our Margaret," Dr. Sabastian said. "I've begged her to stay in town during these holidays, but she insists on going up that mountain. When we found out she was without transportation, we even tried to get her to spend the night with us, but she's stubborn."

Paul looked over at Margaret, who rolled her eyes and smiled, then he turned back to Dr. Sabastian. "The park's a nice getaway during this time of year. Not many visitors during the holiday season, so we're able to give our few guests our undivided attention. Between Joe and some of the other rangers out there, Margaret is well watched over."

Dr. Sabastian put his other arm around Margaret's shoulder and pulled her into his embrace as well. "That's good to know. I guess we'll let you go back then."

Margaret smiled at him and looked as if she would add something, but didn't.

Paul handed her the boots. "You'll need these. It's really cold."

"Thank you for carrying them in. I knew I'd need them." She took the boots from his hand, then walked into the sitting room off from the hall.

"Please, let's go join her," Mrs. Sabastian said.

Paul watched Margaret disappear into the sitting room. "Thank you, but I'll wait here. She won't be long."

Mrs. Sabastian followed Margaret, leaving Paul alone with Dr. Sabastian.

"She tells us that you work at the park."

"That's right. I do." Paul wondered what else she'd told them. For some reason it mattered to him how she'd described him. Just a workman? A friend? Or just a nobody that happened to have a car that ran?

"I've been there for several years," Paul continued. "It's a wonderful place, even this time of year when we're snowed in sometimes."

"Oh, you don't have to try to convince me. We love the park and try to get up there during the spring. I like to fly fish and we spend a weekend or two at one of your cabins along the north shore of the lake."

"Well, you'll have to let me know when you're there so I can make sure everything's okay for you. I usually meet most of the guests, but the spring is pretty busy."

Margaret walked back into the hall wearing her coat and gloves and carrying her little black heels. "Okay, boots and gloves are on. I'm ready to go."

Mrs. Sabastian pulled her close and gave her a hug. "Now, Margaret, if you don't go to Boston, you come spend Christmas with us. Don't you dare sit in that cabin alone."

"Thank you for the invitation. I'll call and let you know, but if I leave, then Joe will be alone. We've gotten to be buddies over the years."

Paul escorted Margaret out to his truck feeling the same as Dr. Sabastian did. He was glad to know someone cared about her well-being. "Looks like the weather's cooperated enough for us to drive back to the park. Are you up to it or do you want a room in town?"

"Oh, no, the park is fine. That is, if you feel like driving that far. It's pretty late."

Paul smiled in the dark of the truck. "I told you, my weekend calendar is empty. Anyway, with a clear sky and a full moon, it'll be a great ride back up the mountain."

The streetlight that stood near the foot of the driveway shone into the truck's interior enough for Margaret to catch the wink he gave before turning around to back out into the street.

To calm the flutter she'd gotten from that innocent gesture, Margaret craned her head to see out the front window. "Oh, my, it is a full moon. Isn't it gorgeous? With yesterday's snow still on the ground and a beautiful sky tonight, this would be a great night for carolers."

"Maybe we'll run into some before we leave town."

All of a sudden she was in the holiday spirit and filled with a giddiness that she hadn't felt in years. "Or, who knows, maybe we'll have a group waiting at the cabin."

His laugh came from deep within his chest. "Uh, I hate to tell you this, but you still don't have a streetlight."

"Or a street." Remembering their earlier conversation on that first afternoon, she smiled.

Exchanging banter with Paul was easy. Had it only been just a week that she'd known this man? How could that be? She felt she knew him better and felt more comfortable with him than a lot of her long-time acquaintances on campus.

He shook his head and exaggerated a frown. "Sorry, Dr. Daniels. No carolers tonight."

## *Chapter Six*

The full moon and the glistening snow didn't let them down. Margaret settled back in the contoured seat and took in the beauty of the mountainside as Paul carefully maneuvered the truck up the steep, sharp curves.

She felt comfortable and safe snuggled on her side of the truck. Paul concentrated on the road, but sat relaxed with one arm propped against the door's armrest and the other hand holding the steering wheel. He looked straight ahead without talking. In fact, he hadn't said much since they'd left town.

"Coming down the mountain you told me I was the quiet one, but going up seems to be your turn."

He looked over with a quizzical expression.

"Quiet? Yeah, I guess I am. I'm really enjoying the view. How about you?"

"You'd have to be blind or oblivious not to enjoy this beauty." She forged ahead, hoping he'd talk with her. "How long have you lived in this area?"

"I'm from around here. I grew up in a small town on the other side of Bluefield. Both of my parents died and the rest of my family's moved on now, except for my sister. I've always wanted to settle down around here."

"So you ventured away for a while."

He nodded, and she caught a hint of a smile. "Yeah, you might say that."

Darn. That was all he offered. Now she was curious.

"So, are you going to tell me where it is that you ventured?"

He waited a second before answering. "All over."

"All over? Exactly what does that mean?" She knew she'd put him on the spot, but she really wanted to know a little more about him.

"Okay, if you must know, I worked overseas for a few years. Had some government contracts in the Middle East while it was still reasonably safe to travel over there. I saw a lot. Learned a lot too." He glanced over at her. "Learned real fast that where you live is not important. It's who you share that space with that makes it important, and I can tell you right now that this is what I want to share with someone. This spot of earth."

Margaret let his words sink in. "That's pretty philosophical coming from someone who didn't like literature."

This time he chuckled. "I didn't need a literature book to teach me that. Life's too short to spend it anywhere except where you want to be and with the person you want to share it with."

"So you plan to stay at the park?" It was an innocent question, but she hoped it didn't sound condescending. The job couldn't pay much, but his new truck showed her that he either had a little money saved from his earlier overseas ventures or he was very frugal. Either way, Margaret saw it as a positive trait.

Money certainly wasn't something she was looking for in a man. Of course, she'd always had enough in her lifetime so she didn't have to worry about something so mundane. She'd never had to live in want. Looking back, she had to thank her father for stressing the importance of being prepared for the future. Margaret knew that with her degrees she'd always be able to support herself.

"Staying with Joe at the park wouldn't be bad."

His words pulled her attention back to him.

"Gives me the time to do what I like to do."

"That would be carpentry," she volunteered.

"Yes. You're a good listener, Dr. Daniels. I like to

do carpentry, and I like doing it in the West Virginia mountains. I like these people. I like the lifestyle. I've moved around a little during my life, but I always seem to end up back here."

He turned and smiled at her, his heavy shadow of a beard now making him look even more handsome than she thought him to be earlier. She cleared her throat. "That's wonderful. Most people aren't so fortunate to know what they want out of life."

"Do you?"

His question caught her off guard. "You mean do I know what I want."

He nodded.

This time she answered in a soft voice. "I thought I did."

What could she add to that? For all her adult life she'd wanted to teach at a college, a small college where she wouldn't get lost in the multitudes. She'd lived her dream for all these years on her present campus, or at least she thought she had. Now the new job offer made her wonder if there was more to life. Had she been living the fulfillment of a dream or was the tiny campus an escape?

Paul maneuvered a curve, then turned his attention back to her. "You thought you knew what you wanted but now you're not so sure?"

She nodded.

"That's not so unusual. In fact, I'd think you're

pretty much in the norm. Most people go through that stage in life. Question where they're going and what they're doing."

She studied his face for a moment. "You don't look like the type to question what you want. I think you knew what your goal was all along."

His laugh was deep. "I do, huh? Well, I hate to tell you but you're wrong. At first I thought I knew what I wanted. When I went overseas I knew that was the right thing for me to do. I could just see me raking in all that money." He tilted his head a little. "And I did, but it wasn't worth it. I found out real quick that money isn't important if you can't enjoy it and . . ." He let his voice drop.

She waited for him to finish, but he didn't. She left the money issue alone even though she really wanted him to continue. "So you didn't like being away from this area."

"Yeah, you might say that. Let's go back to you. You're not sure you want to keep teaching?"

His question startled her. "Oh, no, I don't think I'll ever quit teaching. Being in the classroom fits me. I do think I need to make some adjustments to the way I'm spending my life though."

Margaret nearly gasped when the words came out. From which deep crevice of her subconscious had that come? She had started thinking about getting out more when she was at Dr. Sabastian's gathering tonight, but she'd never consciously made such a strong acknowledgment about changing her lifestyle. Sure, she was thinking about the new job, but did she really need to change other things in her life as well?

Nodding as if he understood, he concentrated on the road, but remained quiet, giving her time to think about what she'd just said.

Had she opened up too much to this man whom she'd just met? How do you tell a stranger that he's partly the reason you're questioning your life? And Paul Reynor *was* a stranger, she reminded herself. She'd known him for less than a week, yet he'd made her question herself as if he'd known her forever.

Maybe it wasn't him at all. Maybe it was time for her to move on and he just happened to appear in her life at the right time to help her see that fact. But even as those thoughts formulated in her brain, she knew they weren't true—or at least not entirely true.

There was something about Paul that Margaret admired, but she couldn't put a finger on it. Maybe it was his relaxed style or his laid-back approach to life, an attitude that was completely foreign to her.

She stared out the window. For her entire life, she'd been told to use each moment to its fullest, to not waste a second. Achieve. Achieve. Achieve. Her A's should have been A+'s. Nothing was ever quite good enough for her parents, especially for her father.

Whew. Now just thinking about her father's words tired her.

Wondering why she'd thought of such things, she cleared her mind and concentrated on the scene outside the window. The banks of old snow against the sides of the road and the little puffs that remained on the trees shone bright white from the moonlight.

Paul drove slowly through the park as if he was in no hurry to get her home. She leaned against the headrest and relished the calm.

When he stopped the truck in front of her doorstep, he leaned against his door instead of getting out. Hating the night to end, Margaret was glad. She wasn't in any hurry to go in either so she turned to him and was about to thank him for the night, but the picture he presented took her breath.

As gentle and calming as she found Paul to be, on the outside there was nothing soft about him. With the moonlight shining into the truck, his eyes picked up a sparkle, but the smile that she'd come to expect had vanished. His expression was serious. His eyes, now almost black in the dim light, held her in his gaze. She didn't move, but felt no discomfort from his stare. It was as if he studied her for a portrait or to understand what she was thinking.

Finally he spoke. "You miss your husband?" His voice was low.

Margaret exhaled a long slow breath before answering. “Of course I miss Edward.”

Now there was discomfort.

She fidgeted with her purse, twisting the tiny strap around her index finger. Looking down, she realized what she was doing and stilled her hands before looking over at Paul. “He’s only been gone for three years. I think of him all the time. Even this place reminds me of him.”

She glanced at him, expecting him to look uncomfortable for bringing up the subject, but he still looked just as relaxed as before. “Yes, I guess it would. Joe told me a little about him. From what he says, your Edward seemed like a very distinguished man.”

She nodded and smiled. “Yes, that he was.”

“How long were you married?”

“Eight years. We married shortly after I started teaching at the college. He was one of the mentors assigned to the new instructors that year and we just seemed to fit.”

“I see. He was like you then?”

“Like me?” She thought a minute. “I’m not sure how to answer that. He was older than I was, very quiet, very studious, and extremely intelligent. He could talk for hours on the history of the Far East. That was his area. He was renowned in the field.”

“I can see where you would fit. You’re smart and from what I can gather, a little on the quiet side.”

"A little?" Margaret had to work to keep from laughing at his assessment of her. "No, Mr. Reynor, I'm not a little on the quiet side. I'm extremely quiet when I'm out of my classroom. I'm not exactly the belle of the ball in a social situation."

"Now, don't you go cutting yourself short. I've never seen anyone as together as you are. I could envision you being right at home at the Mountainside Café where I ate tonight or in an elegant French restaurant."

"You're making fun and that's not nice."

Now he smiled. It spread across his face slicing through the serious façade he had just worn. "I'd never make fun of something like that."

Margaret lifted her purse to her chest in a motion to exit the car. "Let me set you straight. I'm not the belle of the ball now, nor have I ever been. I'm quiet and shy and feel totally ill-at-ease in most social situations unless, of course, they happen to be taking place in my classroom or on campus someplace. I'm very comfortable with my students and with the faculty."

"You don't fool me one bit."

"No, I'm serious. I never even dated before Edward. He was the first man I'd ever gone out with, except for a couple of fixed-up dates that my roommates arranged." She shook her head and laughed. "Horrible memories."

"Oh, yeah. I remember blind dates too. They ought to be illegal."

Margaret laughed and nodded, hoping he'd change the subject from Edward, but he forged ahead.

"So, why do you come up here? If you don't want to think about Edward, I think you'd do better getting lost in the hustle and bustle of holiday shopping and parties instead of spending your time alone."

She sat a minute before she answered. "I tried that scene my first Christmas alone. I hated it. Maybe I tried it too soon after his death." She thought about her words. "Maybe coming up here isn't the right way to get back into life, but it's something that's suited me for the last couple of holidays."

"And now?"

It took a moment for the words to come out. "And now, I don't know, maybe I'm ready for some of the other holiday season again." A chill shook her body.

"You're freezing. I'm sorry. We should've gone right in." He flung open his door and hurried around to her side of the truck. When he opened her door, he offered a hand. The gesture was innocent and unconsciously done on his part, but to her it was intimate and meaningful.

Slowly she reached out and placed her small hand in his big one. With his other, he reached around her and almost lifted her off the seat but without stopping for her to cuddle in his embrace as she had the urge to do. Unlocking the cabin door quickly, they stepped inside together.

The fireplace had kept the cabin from becoming frigid, though it wasn't warm. With the fire burned down to nothing but embers, the light barely flickered. Paul immediately raised the temperature on the electric heater then knelt down by the fireplace. "We'll have this place warm for you in no time."

Margaret removed her gloves as she stood in the middle of the floor and watched him do what he had done that first day she'd met him. "Paul, you've done so much already for me tonight, I feel like I'm imposing. I can do this."

"Nonsense," he said as he positioned several logs on the fire and worked them into a nice flame.

Margaret didn't move. Mesmerized by his actions, she enjoyed his simple act of building a fire.

Finally he stood up and brushed his hands together. "That ought to do it."

"You're not going back down the mountain tonight, are you?"

"No, I told Joe I'd pile up in the spare room. He said he'd make sure I didn't have icicles hanging from the ceiling." He laughed and as he stepped to go past her their arms touched. "I can always count on Joe."

Margaret stepped back quickly, scared that he'd misinterpret her closeness, but then she felt silly. He hadn't even noticed.

With a big smile on his face, he pulled his gloves

back on and stepped near the door. "Do you have any plans tomorrow?"

Dumbly, Margaret shook her head.

"I'm heading back down the mountain and into the valley. If you'd like to take a ride and get away from the cabin for the day, I'd love to have some company. I'll show you what I'm working on."

"Your escape?"

He smiled and nodded. "Yeah. My escape."

"I'd like that."

She reached to open the door for him at the same time that his hand landed on hers. Neither moved. Margaret held her breath. His gloved hand held hers in his. She felt the muscles contracting in his fingers and longed to rip away his glove to feel the warmth of his skin and to feel firsthand the strength and power that radiated from him. For a moment she imagined that strength wrapping around her and keeping her safe.

Finally, he pulled his hand away. She stepped back afraid that he'd read her mind.

"I'll come by around ten to see if you still want to take a ride. It'll be an all-day trek, but we'll plan to eat somewhere along the way. Dress warm and comfortable. We won't be going anywhere fancy."

Swallowing hard, Margaret found her voice. "That sounds great. I'll be waiting."

When the door closed behind him, Margaret stood frozen to the spot as she listened to the sounds of him leaving. What had just happened to her? She closed her eyes and wrapped her arms tightly to her chest remembering the feeling of his hand on hers.

For all these years without Edward, she'd never thought about another man, but tonight Paul dredged up memories that she didn't know how to handle. Closing her eyes, she relished the feeling of femininity, a feeling she hadn't experienced in a long time.

Remembering that her thoughts at the party tonight had ventured into getting involved with the world of the living again, she wondered if that meant letting a man back into her life.

Was it time and was there room to allow another man to share the compartment of her heart where Edward's memory still lingered?

Paul drove slowly toward the ranger station. "Now why did I ask her out?" His words seemed foreign, slashing through the silence in the truck. "You know better than to get mixed up with someone like Margaret." He let that thought settle. Margaret was someone who would never give up the proper society that she was so accustomed to for the kind of life that he wanted.

No, Dr. Margaret Daniels might not know what

she wanted to do with her life, but he knew settling for his lifestyle wasn't in her plans.

"Boy, you'd think I would've learned a lesson with Lydia." Still talking to himself, he shook his head then pulled into the parking lot. "You should leave well enough alone."

He parked next to the station's old truck, turned off the engine, but didn't get out. Sitting alone in the darkness, he knew that he should call her tomorrow and cancel. Make up an excuse. Anything. He didn't need to get involved with anyone, not now when he'd finally found peace in his life. Besides everything that he knew about her, it was obvious she was still in love with her late husband.

For a moment he thought about Edward and hoped that while the man was alive he realized just how lucky he was to have someone like Margaret to share his love.

Paul shook his head. How could he compete with someone like Dr. Edward Daniels, the man who still held the keys to the woman's heart?

Nope, he didn't need to let himself get involved with someone like her, but even as the thought still floated around his head, he knew he wouldn't pay attention to it.

He wanted to take Margaret down to his house. For some reason it was important to him to share what he so loved.

## *Chapter Seven*

Paul turned his truck into a narrow driveway. Two tracks cut through the snow-covered drive with a heavy growth of trees growing along the edges.

"This is it," he said as the truck slowed to a near crawl. "Doesn't look like much now. I haven't gotten around to working on the yard, but after the house is built, I'll have time to concentrate on it. Maybe this spring I'll find a little more time to devote to cutting back all this growth."

Just as Paul had said, he pulled up to her cabin right at ten and drove her down the mountain. In the light of the morning and the warmth of the sun, their banter was light and fun. The deep, somber subjects from the night before were stored away.

Now Margaret sat with her hands folded in her lap

amazed that a driveway even existed in the thick woods they'd come through. "How did you find this piece of land?"

He chuckled. "I kind of fell into it."

She tilted her head and waited for an explanation.

"I was testing a piece of equipment for the county and one of the gears jammed sending me and the tractor over the edge of a small cliff to the east of the property. Nothing was broken on either of us that couldn't be repaired," he threw in before she had time to ask, "but when I opened my eyes, I was looking out over the most gorgeous valley I'd ever seen. I knew right then that it had to be mine."

"So you really did fall into it."

"Yep. Started checking around and found out that a fellow out in Colorado owned it and had no intentions of ever doing anything with it. I made an offer and, voila, here I am. I just couldn't believe someone would own something as wonderful as this spot and not want to live here."

Margaret didn't comment. There was nothing around her but thick bottom growth under tall trees. It was as beautiful as any of the forests around the area, but she saw nothing spectacular about it.

Slowly he drove the truck around a small curve in the road. Now Margaret looked up in amazement. In front of her was a house as magnificent as the forest surrounding it. It sat in a small clearing looking as beautiful as the loveliest Christmas card she'd ever seen. The front porch stretched across the entire width and curved around one side.

Her hand went up to her chest. She spoke softly with a voice she reserved to show reverence in church. "This is beautiful. I haven't seen a wrap-around porch since I used to visit my grandmother in Pennsylvania."

"The house screamed to have a wraparound."

"With a swing," she threw in.

Paul smiled. "With two swings. Get out and we'll walk around the back. The porch extends all the way around the house. I plan to put another swing out there."

Margaret wasted no time in climbing out of the truck. She started to walk through the snow, but he motioned her to follow him. "Come up here. It's finished enough to walk through. You'll get a better feel of the place."

She nodded, then followed him up a makeshift step onto a porch. "Amazing," she said. "You drew these plans and supervised the building?"

Smiling, he shook his head. "No. I drew the plans and I'm following them as I'm building. I've had a little help with the big stuff, but I've done about ninety percent of the work myself."

Stopping, she stared at him. "You built this?"

"Yep. That's why I wanted you to see it. It's what

I do, remember? I said I was in construction at one time."

Intricate craftsmanship along the railings, precision spacing of the boards in the floor as they fanned out around the curve of the house, and solid workmanship told Margaret that this man had a rare, untapped talent.

"Paul, this isn't construction. It's art."

Her words produced a broad smile as he led her around the side porch. "This is my pride and joy." Paul led her onto the back porch overlooking a snow-covered valley. "This is the best feature of the house and I can't even claim it. Mother Nature designed it. I simply decided to borrow it for a short lifetime."

Paul stepped aside and allowed her to stand next to him facing the valley below. For a moment she was speechless. "Oh, Paul, this is the most magnificent view I've ever seen. It's—it's spectacular."

She walked up closer to the railing and leaned into it, drinking in the sight spread out before her. The hillside dropped off into a slope about fifty feet from the house. The snow-covered gully below had small trees scattered along its side. At the bottom a rippling stream cut the landscape in two. Across the gorge was the side of a tree-covered mountain that reached into the clouds. Today the top of the mountain was lost to their view, but Margaret could imagine eagles and hawks soaring overhead.

"I'm in awe. To think, this will greet you every morning of your life after you move in."

Another grin crinkled the skin around his eyes, revealing the pride he felt in his home. "Some days when I finish up here, I pick up my tools then come sit out here alone until the sun goes down."

He pointed off to the west. "The sky puts on a show right between those two ridges at certain times of the year. Sometimes it'll set a little off to the north of it or to the south and you don't get the full benefit, but it's still gorgeous."

Margaret thought a minute. "So how long have you been working on this?"

He shrugged. "About three years."

"Three years? Can't you find anyone to help you?"

This time Paul laughed out loud. "Why would I want to do that? The idea is that I'm building my house the way I want it to be done. It'll be done right, and it'll be what I want."

"But the time—three years seems like a lot of time to put into a house."

"Aah, but that's the issue. It's not just a house. It's a home. My home. Anyway, I'm not in any hurry. Gives me something to do when I'm not up in the park."

She opened her mouth to comment but decided there was nothing she could say that would honor his words. She looked back at the workmanship of the outside walls and smiled. "You're right. This is a home."

That seemed to make him happy. "Come on. Let me show you inside."

Placing his hand on the small of her back, he escorted her through a set of glass paneled double doors. As soon as she stepped through the door, she caught her breath. The workmanship on the outside was spectacular, but the inside was magnificent.

"I'm almost finished with this room. I still have a little work left on the mantel."

"There're logs in the hearth. You use it?"

"Oh, yes. It was one of the first things I finished, and I did have help with the stonework. It was the only way I could work that first winter out here. I have electricity run now, but that winter was a doozy, and I couldn't have survived without the fireplaces."

Margaret stood back and stared at the large stone fireplace that took up about a third of the wall of the room. She stepped closer and ran her hand down the smooth stone in a variety of shades of browns. Many of them sparkled with tiny flecks of blue. "The colors are wonderful."

"They are, aren't they? My friend who's into stonework has connections around here and he helped me pick out the stones for this thing. I think we spent nearly a month after he'd get off work going around to the different quarries to look over their inventory. I knew what I wanted and he wasn't going to be satisfied until we found it."

"You're lucky. We all should know someone like that."

"Yeah. I am lucky. I'd helped him build his house the spring before, so it was a nice payback."

"Well, I'm impressed."

Paul beamed. "Don't be. You don't have to be a rocket scientist to build a house. It just takes patience."

Margaret looked around. "No, you don't, but most rocket scientists couldn't do this. Mr. Reynor, you definitely have been endowed with a rare talent."

Paul stuck his hands in his pocket, an action that she'd come to recognize as a sign of discomfort. "Come on, I'll show you the rest of the house."

Margaret followed him through the remainder of the house. Three large bedrooms with floor to ceiling windows stood empty and unfinished, but it didn't take much imagination to fill in what would be there one day. In the master bedroom another fireplace stood against one wall.

"Oh, what a nice feature. I love my fireplace being so near to the bed in the cabin. I love to watch the flames dance before I fall asleep."

Heat shot up her neck when she realized she'd spoken about so personal a subject with this man, but when he didn't say anything to add to her embarrassment, she continued. "There's nothing better than a real fire, is there?"

"Nope, can't beat it. I'm not taking any chances though. I'm installing a fuel furnace as well as electric heaters in each bath area."

"That's important," she said as she ran her hand along a chair-rail in the hallway. Everywhere she looked, she saw something else that took her breath. Some little nook or cranny that made this project personal and special.

He showed her the rest of the house and finally ended in the kitchen where walls of cabinets stood without doors. "That's what I'm working on this month. It's taking forever to finish the doors."

"I can imagine." She turned to him. "Paul, have you ever considered doing this for other people?"

"You mean working in construction fulltime? Building houses for other people?"

By the look on his face, she knew it wasn't a subject that he wanted to talk about.

"I used to do that. I did that for the government, remember?" He started to say more, but stopped.

She waited, hoping he'd finish his thought, but he only added, "It's not how I want to spend my life."

"But with your talent you could oversee other workers, train them to work to your standards, then sit back and let the money roll in."

"That's exactly what I chose not to do with my life."

"I don't understand."

"No, I don't guess most people would. Let's not talk about it now. Let's just say that I love doing what I do. I love helping Joe at the park, being out in the open, then coming out here where I can work to my heart's content, or not work at all."

She stared at him for a long time. Her father would frown on someone with Paul's work ethic. Where was the drive that was supposed to fill every waking hour of a person's life? Isn't that what her father always preached. She could still hear his words as he stood in front of his massive bookshelves smoking his pipe: "Without drive and discipline, you're nothing. Success doesn't just drop in your lap, young lady. You remember that."

As a young girl, Margaret had lived by those rules, and as an adult she never forgot them. Now she'd give anything to forget them. "So you're content."

"I'm content," he threw in again. "Come on. Let's go out and I'll show you what I have planned for the yard."

For the next hour she and Paul walked around his property with him pointing out places that were special to him and telling her his ideas to make the outdoors as personal as the inside. She didn't have to think hard to envision his plans because they were the kinds of things she too would have done with the area: put a swing hanging from a huge hickory tree limb, a little bridge crossing a small creek at the back of the property, and birdhouses and feeders to keep the yard filled with song in the spring.

By the time they trudged up the last hill and back to the house, he had his hand on her arm helping her. "I'm sorry. I get a little carried away. Did I wear you out?"

"Oh goodness, no. I love to walk. That's one of the things I do when I'm at the park and it's one of my pastimes around campus. I have my little path I go down each afternoon after my classes, and of course, I have my tennis matches and practices a couple of days a week. I try not to let myself get too lazy."

When they got to the truck, he opened the door and reached in. "I know I said we'd go someplace to eat, but Joe suggested I bring along a snack. Would you like to go inside and we'll build a small fire?"

"I'd like that," she said and really meant it. Spending time here in Paul's escape, as he called it, meant a lot to her.

She busied herself setting a small table with paper plates and plastic cups he had stored in one of the unfinished cabinets while he tried to warm the large room. By the time they sat down to ham sandwiches and plastic wrapped snack cakes, the bitter cold had vanished from the room.

The fire was wonderful to watch as they ate. It spread a warm ambiance around the room, but it wasn't the physical cold that was swept away. Margaret consciously admitted to herself that being near Paul took away the cold of her loneliness. She'd missed talking to a man, listening to his thoughts, and simply being with him.

She watched Paul work in his kitchen. "I told you about me," she said as she cleared the table. "It's your turn to tell me about you. You worked overseas in construction. Did you have a wife with you? Children?"

Not looking in her direction, he twisted a tie around a garbage bag. For a moment Margaret thought he wasn't going to answer. "No wife. No children," he finally said, but by his tone, she knew he wanted to drop the subject.

She waited while he wiped the table and spread the cloth on the sink. When he faced her again, he was smiling. "You're not going to let me off, are you? Just like a woman. Got to know every little detail."

Had it not been for the tiny smile, Margaret may have been offended. "That's our job," she said. "Nag the man we're with."

"Okay, let's go. You'll get all the gory details on the way to town."

But the details weren't gory. They were sad, and she was sorry she'd asked.

"Lydia and I were engaged for several years. I

wanted to get married and build us a small starter house on my parents' old property. I had just begun a construction company and it was doing pretty well. She thought we needed to wait until we were financially comfortable before jumping into marriage. She'd come from a pretty well-do-do family, and I think she was afraid I wouldn't be able to provide for her."

Margaret waited, watching him decide how much to tell her. His eyes were on the winding road, but she knew his thoughts were miles away.

"I wasn't a kid. I knew how to make money so I landed some government contracts and spent over a year away from her."

He stopped. A muscle twitched in the side of his face.

She finished what she knew was coming. "So being away didn't make the heart grow fonder, I gather."

He humphed. "For me it did. I couldn't wait to finalize the project and get home, but the projects never ended. Seems as soon as one ended, another was thrown at us. We worked nonstop and would probably still be over there had I not put a halt to it. Made a ton of money, but it wasn't what I wanted. I wanted to get back home to start our life together."

Now Margaret understood how he had gotten the money to build the house.

He inhaled deeply. "I found someone who wanted to buy my company. To make a long story short, selling the company didn't fit into her plans either. I couldn't make the money she wanted around here doing small jobs. She found herself a rich attorney and now lives in one of those massive brick houses with the round columns and concrete all over."

Margaret thought about her family home: cold, sterile, but screaming wealth.

"Sorry I asked." She wanted to tell him that this Lydia sounded as though she should have been her own father's daughter, but she swallowed the words. Whoever had taught Lydia must have come from the same school of life her father had attended.

He glanced at her and smiled, but Margaret could see that the smile didn't reach his eyes. "Don't be sorry. Losing her was a blessing."

Losing someone was never a blessing, even when that person just walked away. She knew the void that Lydia's leaving must have left. "But you never found anyone else to share your dream."

"Nope. Doesn't matter. One day maybe. Maybe not. Life goes on."

"Yes it does, doesn't it?"

He looked at her. "Yep. Life goes on, and that's the way it should be."

* * *

With several hours of daylight still remaining, Paul suggested they take a detour and visit the Mountain Ridge Café. "I'd like for you to meet my friends. While we're in town, you can stop off at campus if there's anything you need to do."

"No, I can't think of a thing I need there." She shrugged. "I have everything I need for the rest of my stay at the park. I'm perfectly content."

"You travel light."

She lifted one shoulder at the same time as one eyebrow. "Yes, I guess I do."

Paul watched her think about her own words. Did traveling light mean she liked to stay unencumbered? Did it mean she didn't want a lot of things cluttering her life? Maybe she just didn't have the energy to bother with too much in her life right now.

Whatever it meant, he allowed her a few minutes of peace and quiet to contemplate what she'd just said.

Finally, he interrupted her thoughts. "You'll like David and Barbara. They're really down-to-earth people. David's dad opened the restaurant, and David just slipped into his shoes and now runs it."

"Did you tell them about me last night?"

She could tell her direct question caught him off guard. "Yes. Certainly. They wanted to know why I was sitting there alone."

She nodded. "And what did you tell them?"

"Here it comes, twenty questions."

She chuckled low. "I told you that was a woman's job. We've got to have all the details."

"Okay, I told them that you're a prestigious professor of English, the head of your department, classy, and beautiful."

She crossed her arms in front of her body and hoped the red she felt creeping up her neck was hidden. "Okay, Mr. Reynor, you're making fun again."

"No, I'm not making fun. That's what I told them, and I meant every word of it."

Was he flirting with her? She swallowed and tried to keep the subject light. "And what did they say to that bundle of lies?"

She watched him struggle for a way of telling her, but she spoke up instead.

"Let me guess," she answered for him. "They said, 'Run for your life.' "

This time he laughed out loud. "Yeah, sort of. That's why I wanted to take you there today. I want them to see that not everyone at the college is sitting up in an ivory tower unaware of what's happening in the real world."

"Hmmm, so that's what they said. I sit around in my ivory tower all day." This time she stared at him a long time. "And how do you know that's not what

I do for the other forty-nine weeks of the year?"

He thought about that for a moment. "Well, if you do, you climb down from it nicely at the end of those weeks."

She laughed and this time the afternoon sun caught a slight dimple in her cheek. "Oh, that's priceless." She laughed again, then got serious. "You know, this David and Barbara might be very perceptive people. Maybe I do use that campus to hide away from the real world. Maybe we all do on campus. I don't know. Sometimes it takes someone on the outside to tell you what you're really doing with your life."

Margaret turned her head and looked out the window and Paul knew the conversation was over. Had he touched on a sensitive topic?

Her laughter had thrilled him, making him remember how nice it was to share an afternoon with someone. Now, though, he felt her sadness and confusion.

"I'm sorry, Margaret."

She turned slowly and looked at him. "Don't be. You were honest and so was I." She smiled again, and he could tell she'd brushed away the momentary melancholy lapse. "I'm looking forward to meeting your friends. I like people who tell you what they think."

"Yeah, well, Barbara might tell you more than you want to hear, but she'd turn around and invite you into her home if she thought that's what you needed. She's a true human being."

"Then I really want to meet her."

Before he knew it, the Mountain Ridge Café sat in front of them. "Still want to go in and meet my frank-speaking friends?"

Margaret picked up her purse and reached for the door handle. "Wouldn't miss it for the world."

After two cups of coffee and the best apple pie Margaret had tasted in years, she and Paul rested against the vinyl seats of a window booth and watched Barbara and David keep the other customers happy.

She hadn't gotten to talk with Barbara yet. With a steady stream of customers, a brief introduction was all the time there was as the woman took their order. So now, they relaxed and enjoyed the warmth of the homey café.

Maybe what Paul had said about the campus professors was true. How had she missed coming downtown to visit this place? Had she locked herself on campus just as she'd hidden out in the cabin for the last few holidays?

For the second time in two days, she made a promise to herself that things would change in her life. It was good to know you were heading in a better direction.

Raising her head, she realized that Paul was staring at her, but before he could say anything, Barbara zoomed past their table and took an order from another customer. "Be right back," she said as she passed.

"Whew, where did all those people come from?" Barbara made her way back to their booth and plopped down on Paul's side. "It never fails. We sit here all morning with nothing to do and all of a sudden we can't catch our breath."

Paul put his arm around her shoulders and pulled her into his embrace. "Yeah, but you live for those days and you can't deny it."

"You're right. We both love it or we'd have sold the joint years ago." She turned her attention to Margaret. "I'm glad he brought you in. I couldn't imagine who was able to make this man sit alone for an entire Friday night."

Margaret opened her mouth to answer, but didn't know what to say to that. She looked at Paul. "Paul, you told me you visited with them all night."

"Well, we sort of visited. They were pretty busy."

"So you sat alone?" Margaret shook her head. "Barbara, this man makes up his mind and there's no changing it. It was his idea to do that last night. I'm sorry if he took up your seating space all evening. I never should have let him waste his entire night waiting around for me."

Barbara laughed. "No, no. It was great. There're a few single females in town who got word that he was in here, and they ended up hanging around for hours. I'm sure they put on a few pounds with all the pie and cake they ate." She laughed. "I guess I shouldn't talk about the women who're after this man."

Paul rolled his eyes. "Don't believe a thing this woman says. Those ladies were old friends."

"Yeah, sure." Barbara turned her attention back to Margaret. "The man won't give any of the female locals a second glance even though he's the best catch in town."

"Okay, this conversation's gone on long enough. Are you ready to go?"

Margaret nodded. "It was nice meeting you, Barbara. Paul has had nothing but wonderful things to say about you and David."

Paul stood up. "We'll stick our heads in the kitchen on the way out to tell him hello."

In an unexpected move, Barbara reached out and took Margaret's hand. "You're welcome here anytime. That campus isn't far from here. You come down and visit with me. Maybe we'll see more of Paul that way."

Margaret nodded again. It was nice to think that Paul would be here more because of her. She tried to extract her hand, but Barbara held on.

"Paul's like family to us." Barbara's words were

simple, her voice low. Nothing else needed to be said. Her indirect warning came across loud and clear. They didn't want their friend hurt.

All the way home Margaret thought about Paul and his relationship with his friends. She was glad that they, Joe, and his sister's family were part of his life. Even though she didn't know Paul well, what she knew of him told her he was a decent man.

She and Paul chitchatted all the way home and when he walked her to her door, she wondered if he'd try to kiss her. They had spent a day and an evening together, and she didn't think it would be out of the question to allow a kiss. Everyone told her that three years was time enough to be a mourning widow. It was time to start letting life happen again.

In fact, she fought a smile that threatened to give her feelings away. She looked forward to kissing him, but when she unlocked the door and turned back to face him, he had backed against the railing a few steps away from her. Margaret had never been good at the dating game, but it was clear he wasn't going to kiss her good night.

Now she swallowed her disappointment. "I had a very nice day. Thank you so much for showing me a little bit of your world. Your house is wonderful, and your friends in the café are great."

"My pleasure." He stood in silence as if he were making a decision. Finally, he stuck his hands in his pockets. "Uh, tomorrow I'm going up to the other side of the park to check on some projects. It's not far from a small private ski slope. I was wondering, if you don't have anything planned, if you'd like to go. Do you ski?"

"Snow ski?" The invitation caught her off guard. "Oh, my goodness. It's been years since I've even been near a slope. When I was younger, my parents had friends who let me tag along with them to the mountains. My parents were older," she threw in, "and they didn't get too far away from the house. Anyway, these wonderful people introduced me to this beautiful park and took me skiing a time or two."

He raised an eyebrow. "Well, would you like to give it a try?"

She inhaled deeply. "I think *try* is the key word here. If you'll be patient, I'll try not to be a burden. I don't have appropriate gear with me though."

"That's not a problem. My friends will have what you need. Can you be ready early again?"

She nodded. With a smile, he headed for the car.

He hadn't tried to kiss her, but he wanted to spend another day with her. That was a good feeling.

When his truck disappeared in the trees, she looked up at the sky. "I do ski, Edward. You just never believed me." She reached for the door, then looked up again. "But that's okay. I love you anyway."

## *Chapter Eight*

"Is there a problem?" From behind the wheel, Paul glanced at Margaret. "You look like you have something on your mind."

Margaret fidgeted. "Maybe."

"Is that all I get is a maybe?"

She laughed. "That's better than telling you that I'm afraid I won't remember a thing about snow skiing. I'd just hate to ruin our day."

Now Paul laughed. "Is that all? I was afraid you'd thought of something else you'd rather be doing."

"Oh, no. I'm thrilled to be out of the cabin again today. You realize this is the third day you've rescued me from my computer screen."

"Is that what I've been doing? Rescuing you? I was afraid I was intruding on your work."

"No, not intruding. Rescuing is more like it."

He chuckled to himself. "How's the writing coming along?"

Now she really laughed. "Horrible. I've worn out the delete button. I can't seem to get anything going, so you really did rescue me."

"Maybe you'll be inspired with a change of scenery."

Margaret nodded, hoping it would help. Since Edward's death, she'd chosen to spend her time at the computer because she had nothing better to do. Maybe she had been pretending to be a writer, just as she was pretending everything was fine in her life.

It wasn't.

Paul's voice pulled her thoughts back to the present. "I want you to know these aren't real ski slopes. It's just a place where some of the locals like to play around. No tourists. Nothing fancy. Just a little snow and a warm fire in a rundown cabin."

"Sounds good to me. I'd hate to compete against some cute little snow bunny on her designer skis."

"No competition there, Dr. Daniels."

His wink warmed her all the way to her toes.

Margaret acknowledged his compliment with only a smile then looked out the side window. The air outside was cold and crisp, but sitting in the closeness of the cab with Paul spread a sense of contentment through her as warm as the morning sun upon her face. She closed her eyes and reveled in the momentary cocoon of security.

This feeling of contentment triggered a barrage of memories—good memories of times she and Edward had shared on similar mountain roads. Usually these bits and pieces of remembrances from their years together saddened her, but today it wasn't like that at all. Those had been easygoing times with a gentle man, times she wanted to remember forever, but life couldn't sustain itself on memories alone.

Opening her eyes, she watched the silent landscape slide by her, caught glimpses of snow-capped fence posts and an isolated mailbox, and knew she didn't want her life to slide by her as well.

She looked back at Paul. "Do you do this often?"

"No," he said with a quick glance in her direction. "I don't come up here a lot. In fact, I don't seem to do much any more than work on my house or help out at the park. I used to ski all the time though."

"With Lydia?"

He humphed. "Yeah, with Lydia, but not up here. She liked the real slopes. We'd go up to Snowshoe together, but she really liked flying out to the western slopes. I brought her up here one time." He chuckled and dropped the subject.

Margaret didn't insist he finish. "I didn't get out on the big slopes the few times I tried. The couple that took me along with them showed me just enough to get by. It was fun just to be out in the open air or to just sit around the ski lodge."

"They sound like good friends."

"Oh, yes. They were younger than my parents. Now that I'm a little older, I can look back and see what they were doing. I think they felt sorry for me. They knew I'd spent my childhood sitting in music halls and lectures with my parents' older friends. I guess in a way they were rescuing me as well."

"Nothing wrong with a little rescuing now and then."

He flashed a smile at her that took her breath away. She'd told him that he was rescuing her from the computer, but she knew it was more than that.

Paul inched his way through a narrow gate then along a small winding road until they came to a log cabin sitting at the top of a slope. Smoke billowed out of two stacks, one on each end of the cabin.

"This is it. No designer skis or fancy restaurants here, but I think you'll like my friends."

From the first introduction, Margaret knew that Paul's friends were good, sincere people and she felt right at home with them. The rustic cabin was larger than her cabin in the park, but the comfortable furniture, big furry rug, and raging fire in the fireplaces made it just as cozy and inviting for her.

With the help of one of the ladies, Margaret tried on several ski outfits, then chose the most comfortable.

With a nod of approval from Paul, she followed him out to the slope. He'd said it wasn't a real slope, but standing at the top looking down, she thought it looked pretty genuine.

She turned when Paul touched her arm. "You're not backing out on me, are you?"

"No way," she said, swallowing her momentary fear. "No backing out now."

"That a girl." He reached down to tighten his bindings, then reached over and adjusted hers.

The innocent gesture on his part sent a tingle of delight through her.

"Do they feel okay?"

Margaret looked down at the slope then back to Paul. "I think so. None of this seems very natural, but nothing hurts, so I guess I'm good to go."

The next two hours flew by in a blur. Cold air rushing across her face. Wet snow clinging to her body with each fall. Quick words of advice from Paul's friends. Lift and tilt. Balance. Breathe.

At one point, Margaret leaned on her poles trying to catch her breath.

Paul slid in beside her on his skis. "You okay?"

He leaned on his poles, but not the way Margaret found herself doing. She was tired and disgusted with her efforts, but he looked energized and excited.

"I'm fine. Just a little disappointed in my progress."

"Hey, don't be. Some people say this is like riding a bike, but I disagree. If your muscles aren't used to this workout, it'll take a little while to catch up. But don't give up. You're doing great."

"I wouldn't say I'm doing great, but I haven't hurt myself yet, so I guess I'll survive."

"I'm going to make one run down the other slope and when I get back up, let's go down together. You rest."

Before she could answer, Paul pushed off. Margaret found a tree to lean against and watched as Paul got into position and attacked the slope not too far from hers. She could see him for the first part of his descent, his big frame positioned as effortlessly as a young teen, his push-off direct and powerful, his descent smooth and flowing.

Margaret watched in awe. The control he showed sent a zing of excitement through her. She, too, wanted to conquer the small slope, to step out of her usual quiet demeanor and do something daring. With a few hours of sunlight left, she watched Paul ski out of sight, then she pushed away from the tree to work on moves foreign to her body's normal workout.

When she finally gathered enough nerve to head down the slope, fear strangled her and kept her frozen to her spot.

She felt Paul come up behind her. "You okay?"

"I think so."

"I'm going down right behind you. If you get into trouble, try to slow down and roll to the ground. I'll be watching you. You're not alone."

His encouragement was all she needed. Determined to do this, she gripped her poles, bit her lip, inhaled and exhaled deeply, then pushed off with a fragment of a prayer on her lips.

The initial descent was slow, but with each successful turn, she found her courage. A feeling of exhilaration swept through her as she set her tempo, established a rhythm, and built momentum.

Margaret felt like a young girl again when she'd dream of doing things that others in her classes talked about or things that she'd read about in books. The quick ski trips with the family friends had helped, but nothing compared to this moment. Each turn seemed to open a window to another world. Each yard that her skis covered left behind a trail of sadness that she'd been carrying around. She felt lighter and freer than she had in years.

By the time she reached the bottom and slowed to a near stop, she couldn't contain the excitement that charged through every part of her body.

Paul slid up behind her. "You did great! In fact, you were fantastic."

She turned to him wanting more than anything to get rid of the cumbersome equipment and throw herself in his arms, but instead she balanced herself and spoke through a grin. "It was fabulous. Exhilarating. The most fun I've had in a long, long time."

His smile said it all. He nodded, then bent down to remove his skis. Before she could do the same, he reached over and helped her.

How long had it been since someone took the time to see to her needs? She could've unfastened her skis alone, but watching him do it sent the same warm feeling throughout her body as she'd had when she watched him build a fire.

"Thank you so much for bringing me up here," she said as he handed her the skis. "This has been just wonderful."

"Yes, it has. I'm so glad you came."

She followed him to the small ski lift. He squeezed in next to her and immediately put his arm around her shoulders. She held onto her skis and leaned into his shoulder.

"If you look over in that direction," he said as the lift carried them away from the bottom of the slope, "you can see the lights of Beckley."

It was hard to concentrate on anything but his arm around her shoulder and his thighs jammed up against hers, but she managed to answer. "It's beautiful. This entire area is beautiful. I'm so lucky to teach so close to all of this."

"And I'm so lucky to live smack in the middle of it."

Glad that he wanted to enjoy the ride in silence,

she relaxed against his shoulder and watched the structures in the distance fade and reappear through breaks in the trees. The cold air nipped her skin as their lift glided just a few feet above the ground.

Looking up, she fixed her gaze on a cluster of clouds and felt as though she were riding the air currents with them. Like a little girl wrapped in the magic of a Christmas tale, she didn't want the moment to end.

Did Paul feel the magic in the air too? She glanced up at him. With his face only inches from hers, he leaned forward and kissed her on the lips. It was a sweet kiss, tender and quick, and when he pulled away, he smiled and tucked her closer to his body.

Neither of them spoke of the kiss—thank goodness. With her blood pounding in her ears and her heart racing in her chest, she couldn't have formed a sensible word. Instead she closed her eyes and relished the feel of his body next to hers.

"How'd it go?" shouted one of the guys waiting for them at the top of the ski lift.

Paul yelled something back to him, then looked back down at her. "I thought it went just fine. How about you?"

"Oh yes, I'd say it was perfect." *Especially the kiss.* She raised her gaze to him and knew he understood.

The rest of the evening flew by. Hot chocolate and a bowl of soup in the lodge. A few funny stories told about the gang's skiing adventures. Cleaning up and storing the ski equipment. It was all part of the others' normal weekend fun, but for Margaret the evening sealed her resolve to find ways to make her life more enjoyable.

As she watched Paul mingle with his friends, she knew she'd like him to be part of that new life she envisioned for herself, but the odds of that happening were slim to none. Sure, he acted as if he enjoyed her company, even kissing her on the lift, but how many park guests did he entertain the way he'd entertained her these past few days?

No, Paul Reynor didn't need a staid English professor in his world. He'd made a comfortable place for himself, and she could only stand on the outside and wish to be part of it. Her father had taught his lessons of life well: Work hard and success will come to you. Well, she'd worked hard, had the best position that a person in her profession could possibly hope for, but watching Paul over the past few days showed her that something was missing in her life.

For the third time since her vacation had started, she made a promise to herself to step out from behind the podium and enjoy life once again.

She'd conquered a small slope today. She was ready to tackle the next obstacle.

## *Chapter Nine*

A hot shower and a borrowed tube of Joe's analgesic cream took the kinks out from her skiing trip. She almost hated to have the soreness disappear. With each muscle ache and stiff joint, she relived the day on the slopes with Paul. It had been the most enlightening day she's spent in years.

Last night when he walked her to her door, the kiss that she'd hoped for the night before became a reality. After unlocking her door, she turned around expecting him to be leaning against the railing again. He wasn't. Instead he stepped next to her, pulled her close, and kissed her with a passion that made her head spin. Too soon, he pulled away and kissed her on the nose.

He was breathing as hard as she was as he opened

the door then stepped aside for her to go inside. "I've got quite a few things going tomorrow, but if I have some spare time, would I be pushing my luck to ask to come by?"

Margaret held the door handle for support and hoped her brain allowed an intelligent answer. "I'd like that."

"Good." He winked, stuck his hands in his pockets, then turned to go to the truck. Before he got off the bottom step, he turned back around and tossed her a tube of cream. "Joe gave me this this morning. Said you might need it."

Now with the cream warming her joints as much as yesterday's memories warmed her heart, she finished her second cup of morning coffee and donned her coat, hat and gloves. She hadn't ventured too far from the cabin alone, but this morning her plan was to hike as far as the waterfall.

Taking a backpack with water, snacks, a small blanket, and a notepad, she hoped relaxing by the falls would inspire a new chapter. Even if she didn't write a word, she wanted to get away from the cabin and out in the open air alone. She had a lot to think about.

After spending the day with Paul yesterday and meeting his friends at the café, she lay awake well into the night trying to sort through her feelings. She had come to the park to get away from the world for a couple of weeks, but now that she was here, the world was finding her. For the first time in several years, she knew she didn't want to close the door on it.

That was one reason she wanted to get away from the cabin. She needed a change of scenery, but most of all she needed to be alone to get her thoughts straight.

She stepped outside but hesitated before turning toward the falls. She had always let Joe know where she'd be, but it seemed silly to walk all the way to the station only to backtrack to the falls. She wished her cell phone worked in the mountains or that she had a phone inside the cabin, but wishing it didn't make it happen.

Making a quick decision, she stepped back inside and jotted a note in case someone needed her before she got back. No need to worry everyone. After jamming it in the door, she felt confident she'd done everything right, then started her morning trek.

Memories of walks with Edward followed her through the small trails and around snow mounds, but this morning they didn't sadden her. She found all the landmarks that he so enjoyed seeing and took time to study the changes to them over the years.

Paul's words came back to her. Life did go on. Hers may have needed a little more of a jumpstart than most women who lose their husbands, but she knew she was well on her way to recovery.

Almost oblivious to the scenery around the trail, she walked deep in thought. Before she realized how far she'd walked, the roar of rushing water brought a smile to her face. Just a couple more turns and she'd be standing next to her beloved falls. She adjusted her backpack and headed out again with a lilt in her step. It didn't last long, however. In the middle of the trail lay a huge tree completely blocking the path.

She crossed her arms and humphed. "Now what?" With the sound of the falls telling her she was just steps away, she had to go on. Examining the fallen tree, she realized there was no way she could climb over it so she studied the area on each side of the trail. One side was so overgrown that she wouldn't dare venture into it. The growth on the other side of the trail wasn't as dense.

"That's it," she said out loud.

Nodding with the satisfaction of making a good decision, she stepped off the main trail. Carefully, looking at each spot where she placed her foot in the snow, she stepped around large broken limbs, but she used the smaller ones for traction. She thought she was making progress but when she looked up to see where she was, she realized that getting around the tree had taken her farther away from the trail and deeper into the brush than she'd anticipated.

She could still hear Joe's warnings from her very first visit up here: "Don't go venturing off the trails.

We don't want to dig you out of a gully. You never know what's under that snow."

Knowing she had to make a slight adjustment in her direction, she took a huge step, but as her foot came down so did a bank of snow next to her. Without anything to grab, she fell to the ground, sliding and tumbling uncontrollably until she and several downed limbs came to a halt at the bottom of a small gully. It had happened so quickly she lay facedown in several inches of snow before she realized she'd stopped sliding. She lay motionless waiting to see if her descent had ended.

Joe had been right, and now she found herself in a predicament.

Snow clung to every part of her body. Her long coat, now twisted and bunched up under her kept most of the wet snow off her body, but it wouldn't for long. She'd be soaked soon, and had to do something.

Terrified that another motion on her part would take her farther down the slope, she moved only her head to survey the area and to see just how much of a mess she'd gotten herself into. The trail with the downed tree wasn't far away from her. She was almost positive that the limbs she could see were from that tree. Feeling better that she hadn't slid down as far as the tumble felt, she inhaled deeply and gave a quick prayer of thanks.

Zeroing in on a half-buried bush that could be

used for support, she decided that would be her first attempt at getting up and out of this predicament. Her right arm lay crooked beneath her body, but as she carefully lifted herself and eased it out, she realized it was fine. She tried to smile at the small victory, but it didn't work. Knowing that she wasn't out of danger, her heart now pounded in her chest.

Calming herself, she grabbed for the bush, but as she extended her body, pain shot up her leg, taking her breath away. "Oh, no, no, no." She groaned and dropped her face against her outstretched arm and waited for the pain to subside.

Finally she opened her eyes. The pain had lessened, but it wasn't going away. The roar of the waterfall that was supposed to invigorate her now only reminded her how far away from the rest of the world she was.

What could she do? Was her ankle broken or sprained? How could she get back to the cabin if she couldn't get up? Frustration and her first acknowledgment of fear nearly gagged her. Her hands shook, she could hardly catch her breath, and her leg throbbed unmercifully. Why had she come out here alone? Why hadn't she waited and asked Paul to escort her?

Thinking of him eased her fears for a moment. He would probably be back in the park by now and, if he kept up his daily routine, he would go by her cabin to check on her. She prayed he would. "Please come look for me, Paul. Please."

Paul stood on Margaret's front step with the note in his hand. Fear gripped his throat like a vise. She'd gone to the falls, but she'd gone this morning. He looked at his watch: 4:17. It would be getting dark within the hour.

Where was she? Why wasn't she back?

His first instinct was to rush off through the park to find her. Knowing she could be lying somewhere alone in the snow pulled at his heart. He held back. Before rushing off down the trail, he had to go back to the station. Joe needed to know what was happening to be ready to call for backup if it was needed.

He made himself stop for a moment to think. He should pick up some other supplies and another walkie-talkie to keep in touch with the cabin.

He prayed he was wasting his time. He wanted more than anything in the world for Margaret to be sitting in Joe's rocker sipping a cup of tea.

She wasn't.

With a few instructions to Joe, Paul stuffed a flashlight, a blanket, water, and a small knife into his backpack, then ran out to his truck and drove as close as he could to the waterfalls. Checking his supplies once more, he started out toward the falls. First he'd check nearer to the falls, then if he didn't find Margaret there, he'd walk the rest of the trail back to the cabin looking for her.

He stood quietly and listened. He could barely make out the sound of the water pouring over the falls, but nothing else stirred. He called her name. Called it again. Nothing.

Inhaling a ragged breath, he plowed down the trail. Several pairs of footprints broke through the clean snow, and the smallest set looked freshest. They had to be Margaret's. He called out again.

For ten minutes he followed the footprints, calling her name, then stopping to make out a sound. The roar of the falls got louder making it harder for him to hear or for her to hear him. He yelled louder.

Finally, he stopped and strained. Was that a voice? "Margaret!" he shouted. "Margaret, are you out there?"

Again he stopped and listened. He swore he heard the whisper of his name but with the noise of the falls, he couldn't tell from where it was coming. The footprints continued down the trail. So did he. When he came to the tree lying across the trail, he swallowed hard envisioning what she must have done. Footprints leading around the tree told him what he'd feared.

"Margaret, answer me if you hear me."

He stopped, straining to hear.

"Paul." This time he was sure he'd heard something. He ran through the snow until he saw where the footprints slid into a gully. His heart raced. He stepped to the edge, held his breath and looked down. Several yards down into a shallow gully, he saw a mound of white with a hand waving to him. "Thank you, God. Thank you," he choked.

Quickly, he pulled out the small rope, wrapped it around the nearest tree, then carefully found his footing as he inched his way down the slope.

"Don't move, Margaret. Don't move." He couldn't make out her mumbled words, but just hearing her voice sent a thrill through his body.

Finally, he knelt by her and carefully lifted her head. Her weak smile brought tears to his eyes. The lump in his throat kept him from saying anything. She lay on her stomach but with a groan turned into his arms.

As he lifted her, she grabbed for his neck. He pulled her close, held her tight, then kissed her on the lips. They were cold and dry.

Pulling her body closer to him, he felt her shiver. She was freezing. He knew he had to do something, but first he had to hold her.

"I was so worried," he whispered.

Through sniffles, her voice shook. "Me too." She pulled away enough to look into his eyes. "But I knew you'd come."

He nodded, then reached for a canteen of water

and placed it to the lips he'd just kissed. "Are you hurt?"

"My leg. I think I twisted my ankle. I don't think it's broken though. I crawled a little ways," she said in between swallows, "but it hurt too bad. Scared I'd make it worse." She squeezed his hand that held the canteen. "I had water in my backpack, but I don't know what happened to it. I've been eating snow." She tried to laugh, but several tears slipped down her cheeks.

Gently, Paul placed her head back on the ground. "I'll look for your backpack in a minute, but let's take a look at that leg."

He turned his attention to the swollen area above her boot. The snow boot still covered the ankle, but he could tell it was cutting her circulation.

He looked up. "I'm going to cut your boot. You need to get some blood to that area."

She nodded but he could sense the fear in her face.

"You'll be okay. We'll have you safe and warm before you know it." He talked while he cut away the rich leather, knowing she needed reassurance, but mostly to hide the trepidation he was feeling. What would have happened to her had he not gone by her cabin before leaving the park? He shuddered at the thought.

Once he had cut away the boot, he wrapped her in the blanket from his backpack.

He found the walkie-talkie, let Joe know what was happening and told him to call an ambulance.

"I feel so stupid," she whispered as he gathered things to leave.

"Well, don't. This could happen to anyone. I'm just glad you're okay." He swallowed hard and tried to offer her a smile. Looking around, he spotted a dark spot several feet above where she lay. "I think I see your backpack. I'll be right back."

He left her only for a moment as he retrieved her pack and her hat lying near it. He showed her the hat. "Did you have anything else with you?"

She shook her head.

"Okay, my truck's not too far from here. I think I can carry you without hurting your leg. Are you game?"

"I've been waiting for you to say that. I'm more than ready." Without her hat her hair lay in a tangled wet mass, but the smile she gave him was hopeful, and to him, she was beautiful.

Carefully he placed his arms under her and lifted. She wrapped her arms around his neck and held on while he pushed himself up. Even with the heavy coat, she felt light.

She buried her face in his coat and gripped the back of his neck.

"Am I hurting you?"

She shook her head, but didn't answer. She didn't

need to. He could tell she was uncomfortable, but there was nothing more he could do.

"Hang in there. We'll be at the truck before you know it."

Later, Paul didn't remember much about getting back, nothing, that is, except holding Margaret in his arms and having her slender arms wrapped around his neck and her body snuggled against him. By the time they reached the truck, the perspiration on her face told him she was in a lot of pain, but she hadn't said a word or whimpered. She simply held onto him for dear life.

And for that moment, their clinging to each other *was* life itself. Maybe it was the hyped up adrenaline or the fear of finding Margaret injured that had his emotions on edge, but all Paul knew was holding this woman in his arms meant more to him than anything or anyone else had in a long, long time.

Ever since she'd opened the door to her cabin that first evening and let him in, he'd known there was something special about her. He felt it that first day but had told himself he was being ridiculous. She was a stranger, someone living in a different world from his own, and someone who was still in love with her dead husband.

But today, as he searched for her through the woods, he knew he couldn't deny his feelings. He didn't give his love easily, but he wouldn't turn his back on it either.

"Margaret, we're at the truck. I need to put you down. Keep the weight off your hurt leg."

Margaret opened her eyes. "I don't want to let you go," she whispered. "I feel . . ." but she didn't finish.

Paul looked down at her and swallowed, almost losing himself in her big brown eyes. "It'll be just for a second. I have to open the truck and adjust the seat for you. I won't let you go."

The last few words were innocent, but they packed more truth in them than he dared to admit.

Lowering her body gently, he helped her stand on one leg while she held onto him with both her arms. This time she did whimper, squeezed her eyes, and groaned.

"It's almost over." After getting the seat back, he lifted her once more into the seat, but before she relaxed against the back, she pulled him to her and buried her face in his neck. Feeling her tears run down his skin, he held her tight and let her cry. She deserved to. She'd been through a lot.

Finally, she inhaled a long breath and pulled away just enough to see him. "I'm sorry. I never cry. I'm just so happy to be here with you. I was so scared."

Paul pushed her hair back and kissed her lightly on the forehead. "Don't you ever be sorry for being scared or happy or emotional. You're human. You're allowed to cry a little, especially after what you just went through. You kept your cool out there, and I don't know that many people could've done that."

This time she smiled and lifted her head enough to kiss him gently on the lips. "I don't know how cool I was. I just know I've never been so glad to see anyone in my entire life. Thank you for coming for me."

Paul nodded, laid her back against the seat, and buckled her in. "That's so I don't lose you."

If only that were so, he thought.

Margaret lay against the leather upholstery and pulled the blanket tighter around her chest. The heater in the truck rapidly spread warmth through the cab, but the trembling she felt in her body wasn't from the cold. Knowing what could have happened scared her to death.

Had Paul not come for her, would she have been able to make her way out of the woods? She doubted it. She'd dragged herself halfway to the trail where he'd found her, but she was certain she couldn't have pulled herself all the way to the cabin. The pain and the damp cold had sapped her strength.

Paul drove faster than he normally did through the park. He sat quietly behind the wheel, his face serious, his hands gripping the steering wheel. She had told the truth when she'd said she couldn't think of being happier to see anyone. When he'd walked up to her and lifted her head in his hands, it was as if all her prayers had been answered.

Not only had he saved her from a fate she didn't want to think about, but she knew he'd come because he cared.

Maybe it was his job at the park to save stranded visitors, but it wasn't his job to check on her each night. He pretended that it was normal procedure, but in her heart she knew it wasn't.

What did it all mean?

She liked watching him maneuver the dark narrow trail, but the heaviness of her eyelids was too much to fight. Closing them, she let the weight of the world float over to Paul's side of the truck. It felt good to let someone else shoulder the burden for a little while.

## *Chapter Ten*

The truck stopped, a door slammed, and voices surrounded her, but Margaret had a hard time tuning in to the turmoil. A whoosh of cold air hit her. She shivered.

A warm hand touched her face. Paul's hand. She reached up and held it.

"Margaret, we're back at the station. The ambulance is at the entrance of the park already so I'm not going to take you out of the truck. Are you warm enough?"

His words floated in and out, but she managed to open her eyes. "Don't leave me."

He slid into the seat with her and closed the door. Snuggling up against his jacket, she smelled its woodsy scents, but mostly she inhaled Paul. He smelled masculine. Turning into his body, she cuddled closer. She knew this moment wouldn't last, and she wanted to take as much of him with her as possible.

"I hear the sirens," he whispered into her hair. "The ambulance will be here in just a minute."

Margaret opened her eyes and looked up. "Just take me to the cabin. I'll be okay."

His face was inches from hers. He lowered his lips to hers and kissed her lightly. She pulled herself closer, letting him kiss her again, then moaned when he pulled away and tucked her head beneath his chin.

"Your teeth are chattering."

She tried to answer but wasn't sure the words actually formed. "Not g-good to kiss with ch-chatters."

Nothing seemed right. Her mind was muddled. Her body shivered, but being in Paul's arms felt cozy and safe.

"You need to get checked out," he said as he stroked her hair. "That leg needs x-rays."

The other door opened and a rush of cold air pushed her closer into Paul's jacket.

"They're almost here."

It was Joe's voice.

Margaret tried to turn her head. "Joe?"

"It's me, Mrs. Daniels. You're going to be just fine. Those ambulance people made it up the mountain in record time. I told them they'd dab-burn better not waste even a minute."

She felt him place a hand on her shoulder, but unable to turn her head, she smiled into the red plaid jacket.

The next few hours were a series of blurs. Someone lifted her onto a stretcher and tucked warm blankets around her. It felt good, but the only warmth she wanted was Paul's. She opened her eyes to find him, but only saw the top of the ambulance. Lots of hands touched her at once. Someone inserted a needle in her arm while someone else wrapped warm things around her legs and arms.

Sirens cut through the night, but even they sounded as if they were somewhere else, somewhere over the other mountain hauling some other poor soul off to the hospital. She hoped that person would be okay. Right now she couldn't ask who was being transported. She needed her sleep.

More hands lifted her. She knew they did, but without being able to open her eyes, it was impossible to see who did it. She didn't question it, simply enjoyed the ride on whatever it was they had put her on.

Finally a bright light seared her eyes. "Oooh, bright."

"Well, hello, Dr. Daniels. We were wondering when you'd join us."

Margaret looked up into the face of two men and three women, obviously nurses and doctors, and it hit her—she had been the one being taken to the hospital. She had been the one injured.

She groaned. She wanted to say something but her mouth was so dry the words didn't come. As if the nurse knew, she placed a small ice chip in her mouth.

"Thank you," she said when she was able to form the words. "Have I been here long?"

One doctor spoke up. "Oh, long enough for us to figure out that you're going to live." He smiled big. "I'm Dr. Madison and you're at the Blue Ridge Valley Clinic. We might be small, but we're good. You won't get more personalized care anywhere."

Another big smile.

"Thank you." She looked around. "Is my ankle okay?"

"Oh yes. You're a lucky lady. A little more pressure and you would've had a nice break. As it is, you managed to get yourself a small hairline fracture that'll heal like new if you'll stay off of it for a while."

"I can do that."

"We'll get you to your room. You'll be with us overnight just for precautions."

She frowned and wanted to argue, but didn't have the strength.

"We don't want you to come down with pneumonia, do we?"

Shaking her head, she closed her eyes once more and hoped they'd finish whatever they needed to do with her before she awoke again.

Paul leaned against the wall in the hallway outside the examination area of the Emergency Room.

Joe sat on one of the cushioned chairs in the waiting room not far from him. "Why don't you come over here and sit? Standing closer to that door won't get you answers any quicker."

Paul looked at Joe and had to agree. He'd been standing there for over an hour catching a quick glimpse of Margaret as they moved her about in the examining room. He knew they'd done x-rays and had her checked out by now, and he was antsy to hear the results. But what Joe said was right. He wasn't doing anyone any good by taking up hall space.

He walked to the coffee stand, poured himself another cup, then stretched his legs as he sat across from Joe. "I hate waiting."

Joe chuckled. "Yeah, well, it's nobody's favorite pastime."

"I should've made you stay at the station. There's no reason why we both need to be here."

"Yeah, and you could've stayed up there too. I could've followed the ambulance." Joe raised his eyebrow and waited for a response.

"Okay, you got me. We both wanted to be with her."

Joe fidgeted. "Think we ought to call the people she visits on that campus?"

"The Sabastians? We probably should, but not tonight. I'll let them know tomorrow."

Paul sipped his coffee and wondered if she'd choose to go to their house to recuperate or if she'd want to go back to the cabin if her leg wasn't too bad. The Sabastians would be the perfect solution for her, but selfishly he hoped she'd want to be in the park where he could take care of her.

Taking the last sip of coffee, he crumpled the cup and tossed it in the can.

Thinking she'd want him to take care of her was a stupid idea. He'd already let himself get too close to her, and he knew he'd feel the void when she returned to campus. The park was a distraction for her—nothing more—and he was afraid that's the way she looked at him as well. Oh, he knew she enjoyed being around him, even liked his kisses today, but then, he'd saved her life.

If he closed his eyes, he could still feel her soft lips against his, her hands clinging to his neck, and the tears that touched his skin. Knowing she was in danger had ripped through him with an emotional force that he hadn't experienced in a long, long time.

He should never have kissed her, but he couldn't help it. When she returned his kiss, he discovered something he thought he'd never feel again.

But kiss or no kiss, he'd have to get her out of his head and definitely out of his heart because he had a feeling her kiss was just a response to the moment. She was emotional and almost out of her head, grateful to have anyone carry her back to safety.

But then he thought about the kisses the day before. How did she feel then? He was afraid he wouldn't want to know the answer.

Nope, to the Sabastians she'd go to heal, and he'd figure a way to get her out of his system.

Joe stood up and walked to the window. "Well, I can see you're going to be the brilliant conversationalist while we wait."

Paul was glad to have a distraction. "Sorry. I guess I was just deep in thought."

Joe turned around, scratched his chin and humphed. "I've seen a possum on alert with more response than you've had in this waiting room."

Paul wanted to defend himself, but when he looked at Joe, he realized that the old man was just as nervous as he was. His drawn face and taut lips couldn't hide the tension that he felt. Joe had known her for a lot longer than he had, and the love he had for her was obvious.

But their wait wasn't long. Before Paul had a

chance to defend his quiet demeanor, the doors to the off-limits area swung open. One of the young doctors came out with a smile on his face. Immediately Paul swallowed the lump that had formed in his throat.

Margaret would be okay. She'd be kept overnight for observation, but they could see her when she was settled in her room.

Paul listened, nodding dumbly, but Joe spoke up several times and asked the right questions for them to know they could take her home tomorrow.

As the doctor swept back through the swinging doors, Paul and Joe both stood unmoving and watched the doors come to a stop.

"Good news," Joe finally said after a quiet sniffle.

Paul nodded and swallowed a lump of emotion blocking his airway. "Yep. Real good news."

The clinic had only one wing of rooms on the bottom floor, and as Paul and Joe made their way to Margaret's room, both said very little. Paul kept his eyes on the immaculate tiles, trying to figure out why he'd gotten so emotional. The lady would be okay. He and Joe should've hit each other on the back, made a wisecrack, then gone out for a drink to celebrate her good luck.

But they didn't. Margaret Daniels's accident had touched them both as nothing had in a long time. Paul felt it, and he knew Joe had as well.

Before they reached Margaret's room, both men lifted their heads and straightened their shoulders. Joe turned to Paul. "She's a special lady. She's brought a little zing to your walk that I haven't seen in a long time. Don't let her get away."

"Now don't go playing matchmaker on me. She's special, but that doesn't mean we're right for one another, so . . ."

"Oh, phooey. What does that mean? Who decides what's right?"

Joe pushed open the door to her room and left Paul standing in the hallway.

Yes, Margaret was special. Yes, he felt something with her that he hadn't let into his heart in a long time, but his world and Margaret's world were so totally different that he had no false ideas or hopes that there would ever be a neutral ground on which to meet.

He was just relieved that she was okay. As far as the rest, he wasn't totally confused. He now knew that his first impression of Margaret had been wrong. She had the outward trappings of someone living in an elite world secluded from the humdrum of the working class, but there was more to her than that.

The sophistication that was a natural part of her past life and job was only a small part of who she was. She was genuine and fun-loving, not condescending and boring as she could have been. He liked that. How had he ever compared her to Lydia?

Paul knew Margaret would fit into his world if she'd give it a try, but would it be fair to ask her to give up what she so loved?

The answer shouted loudly in his head. She had a life, a good life, and what he'd chosen to do with his would take her away from what she loved.

Margaret lay in the hospital bed waiting for the first light of morning to peek through the sides of the window blinds. The sleep medication the nurses insisted she take had worn off hours ago. Now she lay awake rehashing the last twenty-four hours.

Forgetting the entire incident would've been a blessing, but with a bum ankle confining her to the bed and the remembrance of kisses still warming her lips and her heart, she knew the last two days would be forged in her mind for a long, long time.

Would Paul come back today to check on her? Would he still have that look in his eyes that hinted at more than a dutiful rescue by a friendly park ranger? Would he be embarrassed that he'd kissed her again? And how did she feel about returning his kiss?

Maybe she'd been so terrified by the time he found her that she imagined his emotional response.

Of course he would have been ecstatic to see her. It was his duty to find her.

She squeezed her eyes shut. There was more to what she saw in his face and felt in his arms than just duty. There was real feeling there, not like the little kisses the day before.

She might have been helpless on the trail, but she hadn't been delirious. She hadn't.

Punching her pillow against the curve of her neck, she moved her leg to get into a more comfortable position, then grimaced. The soreness and the stiffness in her ankle seemed worse this morning. Darnit.

Walking out of this facility on her own two feet was probably impossible. She hated to be dependent on anyone, and now she lay in the bed not even able to walk down the hall alone. "Darnit. Darnit. Darnit." This time the words bounced off the walls.

Closing her eyes, she wallowed in self-pity for a few minutes. She had to get it out of her system before she faced the day. She would never face her friends in this condition. She'd face them with a smile on her face, or else. . . .

She laughed at that thought. Or else what? Feeling better, she let the heaviness in her eyelids take over.

"Good morning, Dr. Daniels."

A nurse swung through the door carrying a tray of instruments, then walked over to the blinds and opened them. "After all that snow we've been having, this morning is gorgeous. We can't have you not seeing that wonderful sunshine, can we?"

Margaret blinked against the bright sunshine, but was thankful that she'd fallen back to sleep and the night had finally ended.

For the rest of the morning, nurses came and went in a whirlwind of activity. The doctor who had worked on her leg came by. Breakfast was brought in and papers were shoved in front of her to scribble a signature.

She was ready to go home, wherever that was.

The discharge nurse told her that arrangements had been made, but she wasn't sure who was supposed to pick her up. Margaret smiled.

"Now don't you worry, Dr. Daniels. Someone will be here to pick you up by the time we have you all ready."

So with anticipation, Margaret sat on the side of the bed and waited to see who would come through the door for yet another rescue. She crossed her fingers that it would be Paul, but deep in her heart she felt sure it wouldn't be. The man had a job to do in the park. He couldn't baby-sit every helpless female guest who needed him.

A tiny knock pulled her attention to the door as the Sabastians tiptoed into her room. She smiled at their serious faces.

"Aren't you a sight for sore eyes," she said and hoped her disappointment didn't show.

Mrs. Sabastian came over and placed an arm around her and kissed her on her cheek. "We would've been here sooner, but Mr. Reynor just called us a few hours ago. It took that time to make sure the spare room was fixed up and comfortable for you."

She swallowed her disappointment. "So I'm going to your house?"

Dr. Sabastian crossed his arms. "Yes, and we won't listen to any of your complaining or assuring us that you can manage on your own."

Swallowing the hurt that Paul hadn't bothered to come by to help her leave, she lifted her head. "Thank you. I'd love to go sit in front of my fire in the cabin, but I won't argue. I know that's impossible. It would make life difficult for everyone else. I guess I'm all yours."

It would be useless to complain. These were her friends, and she'd show her appreciation.

With the help of two nurses, Margaret was bundled into the back of Dr. Sabastian's sedan. With a wave to the staff and a quick survey of the parking lot for a familiar black truck, she left the clinic with a heavy heart.

"I have to confess," Mrs. Sabastian said as her husband pulled away from the clinic, "we went into your campus apartment and packed you a small bag. I know most of your things are at the cabin, but no one had time to get them here this morning. Mr. Reynor assured us he'd be back down here sometime today with some things for you."

What could she say? Paul would do his duty to get her the things he thought she needed, but in her heart she knew he had no idea what she truly needed. No one did.

Mrs. Sabastian chattered away as Margaret watched the small town flit by her window. Snow piles were pushed alongside the roadways in their usual winter appearance, but they looked different to her today. At the park, the snow was clean and fresh, untouched by man and cars. Here dirt from the tires blackened the ugly piles.

She turned her face away.

"With Christmas just two days away, we assume you'll still be with us through then. We're just thrilled. None of our children are able to drive up this year. This will be wonderful to have you in the house with us."

Margaret nodded, surprised at the emotion that threatened to blur her eyes with tears. Christmas with the Sabastians? It wasn't what she'd planned for herself, but she'd have to pay for her stupidity of walking to the falls alone.

Holding Margaret's suitcase in his hand, Paul rang the doorbell and waited as he'd done just a few nights before when he'd picked Margaret up from the party.

Now he was carrying her clothes so she could stay in town while he was in the park or at his place miles away from her.

It wasn't what he wanted to do.

Mrs. Sabastian opened the door and grabbed his free hand. "Come in, Mr. Reynor. Come in."

"Thank you, Mrs. Sabastian, but would you please call me Paul?"

"Why certainly, Paul. Let me take your coat and you can go up the stairs to visit with Margaret. I'm sure she'll be glad to get her own things. First room on the right."

He looked at the massive staircase. "How did you get her up there?"

"My husband almost carried her, but we made it okay. She did just great. This is a fine house, but it's built for entertaining. There isn't a bedroom downstairs."

Paul made his way up the stairs trying to take in the beautiful workmanship as he'd done on the first night he was here. This morning, however, his mind wasn't on construction or talented nineteenth-century carpenters. It was on a woman who lay up in a bedroom alone.

At her door, he took a deep breath, knocked, then waited.

"Come in."

Opening the door a crack, he stuck his head in. "Hi. You up for a little company?"

Margaret lay on her back in the bed with her leg propped up underneath the blanket. "Please come in and save me. I'm not one to lie in bed all day."

Paul laughed as he stepped in. "No, I don't imagine you are."

He walked over to the bed, reeling in the urge to crawl in alongside her and pull her into his arms.

"Did you come to rescue me again?"

"Oh no, from what I gather from the doctors, you need to stay right where you are for a couple of days."

She twisted her lips. "That's what I'm told, but I can still hope."

"You can hope all you want to, but you'll have to stay put for a little while." He lifted the suitcase. "I brought you a few things that Mrs. Sabastian suggested. Joe and I went into your cabin. Hope you don't mind."

Margaret laughed. "No, I guess everyone now knows what an awful housekeeper I am. She got into my apartment on campus and brought a few things too. How embarrassing. I just hope I had everything picked up. I can be pretty messy sometimes."

Paul placed the suitcase down then pulled up a straight-back chair closer to the bed. "You're anything but messy. Everything looked neat so don't worry about us seeing anything out of place."

"Thanks for bringing my things. That was very thoughtful of you."

He nodded, but looked around the room, needing to pull his eyes away from Margaret. Lying flat on the bed with her hair spread out across the pillow, she looked young and vulnerable and in need of being hugged.

"Can you help me sit up a little?"

He swallowed. The last thing he needed to do was to touch her, but he couldn't ignore her request. Standing up, he leaned over and wrapped his arms around her shoulders, lifting her and positioning the pillow in one careful motion. He tried to ignore the fact that her arms had reached around his neck just as she'd done on the trail back to the truck. With warm fingers, she clung to him and even after he'd placed her back on the pillow, she kept her hands around his neck.

Unable to control himself, he gave in to the urge and relaxed, placing his head next to hers on the pillow, his lips in her hair. "You had us all worried."

"I'm sorry," she whispered. "I have to admit I was scared to death."

He pulled her closer and lifted slightly, then kissed her on the lips. Whether it was relief from knowing she was okay or the response of her kiss to him, a surge of need rushed through him, taking his breath away. With his heart pounding in his chest, he pulled away quickly before he did something stupid like tell her he loved her and couldn't live without her.

He sat up and got his control. He was sure she was unaware that the flushed area around her mouth and her half-closed eyes invited him to kiss her again. He needed space. He stepped away from the bed and sat in his chair.

"I'm sorry I worried everyone," she finally said. "And I'm sorry I was so stupid to try to walk around that tree. I don't know why I did. I know all the rules of the park."

"That tree shouldn't have been blocking the trail. It must've fallen the night before. No one reported it or it would've been removed or the trail would've been closed. Joe and I feel like some of this is our fault."

"No, it's not your fault. You and Joe keep a close eye on the grounds, don't you?"

"We try, but we're not alone. There's a skeleton crew even during the Christmas holidays. We let our other guys go work up at the ski slopes so they can make a little extra. This is the busy time for them. It's pretty slow for us."

Margaret nodded, but didn't add any more.

"They let me see you for a few minutes at the hospital last night."

Her eyes widened and he knew she hadn't remembered.

"You were pretty doped up. You had just been moved into your room, then they ran us off and told us the best thing for you would be sleep."

"Thank you. You and Joe went beyond the call of duty. I'm sure most of your park guests don't cause half the trouble that I have."

Paul couldn't fight the smile that spread across his face. "Yeah, but they're usually not half as pretty as you are."

"Now you're embarrassing me."

"Didn't mean to. Just telling the truth." What he hadn't told her was that he'd lain awake the entire night worrying about her, blaming himself for her accident, and wanting to be with her at the hospital.

How had it happened that a park guest had touched his life so deeply in just the two weeks she'd been there? And more importantly, what would he do about it?

Long after Paul left the house, Margaret lay awake reliving his kiss and what he'd said. The kiss had been quick and the words had been few, but they would be imbedded in her memory forever.

After all the years she'd worked with students, she was good at reading people, and after watching Paul for the few minutes of his visit, she knew there was something that he wasn't telling her.

She could feel it, and wondered if she'd ever find out what it was. The more she got to know Paul, the more complicated he became. She wished with all her heart that she would have more time with him. There was so much she wanted to know. For now though, she snuggled under the covers of the Sabastians' bed and wished she was looking at her fireplace in the cabin.

## *Chapter Eleven*

Christmas morning found Margaret still in the bed upstairs in the president's house on campus. She'd gotten up and walked a little over the past couple of days, but today she was determined she would get up, put on a little makeup, and dress for Christmas dinner.

That was easier said than done.

After almost a two-hour episode of getting herself ready, she had to lie down across her made bed to get back her energy.

When she opened her eyes, she realized she'd fallen asleep. "So much for being a help in the kitchen today."

With the smell of turkey and dressing wafting up the stairs, she grabbed a borrowed cane and hobbled down the stairs fighting a growling stomach and an aching ankle.

"Well, look who's joining us this morning."

Dr. Sabastian jumped up from his easy chair and met her halfway down the staircase. "Glad you decided to be a little ambitious today." He yelled over his shoulder, "Judith, come see who's back in the world of the living."

"Merry Christmas," Margaret said as he helped her down the last few stairs. She gave him a fatherly kiss on the cheek. "I'm feeling much, much better. Just getting up and dressing did wonders for me." She didn't mention the fact that it had taken her all morning to get herself together and required a nap afterward.

He led her into the kitchen where Judith was basting the turkey. With a full apron tied around her body, she reminded Margaret of her nanny when she'd grown up in her parents' home.

What a strange thought. Most people would associate that homey appearance with their mother or grandmother, but not Margaret. She remembered very little about her grandparents who had died when she was a little girl. Her mother, older than those of her classmates, never filled in the gap with warm memories of baking cookies or decorating cakes.

Up until her parents' death, there had always been maids and housekeepers and nannies to do the mundane chores. She wondered if her well-meaning parents had warped her in some kind of way. What a heyday a psychiatrist would have with her!

With a near smile from that thought, she plopped down in a chair by the kitchen table. "Whew. That was a chore." She lifted her leg and propped it on a small stool that Dr. Sabastrian produced. The couple fussed over her until she held up her hand.

"I'm comfortable. Thank you."

They looked at her expecting her to collapse.

"I promise. I'm fine. In fact, I had intentions of coming in earlier and helping you, but it took me a little longer to get ready than I thought it would."

That seemed to satisfy both of them. Dr. Sabastian patted her head and left the two ladies alone. Judith turned to the cabinets and talked while she pulled out a coffee cup.

"I enjoy doing this. I don't cook much anymore. Harold and I eat out a lot. Seems we always have a dinner engagement connected with the college. If that's not the case, then our housekeeper makes something up before she leaves. Harold's schedule just doesn't allow us the domestic time we'd like. Oh, no. I don't need any help. I love doing this."

Judith poured a cup of coffee and set it in front of Margaret. "Thank you."

"We're going to eat our Christmas dinner in about an hour. We like our big meals in the middle of the day. I guess as we get older, our stomachs demand attention earlier."

Judith's laugh lit an answering smile in Margaret. Margaret felt good about being here. She settled back, sipped her coffee, and watched Judith get the meal together. For only a moment she allowed a melancholy thought to grip her heart as she remembered Edward's last Christmas with her. He'd been sick and only nibbled on the huge meal she'd prepared.

Pushing that thought away, she talked about other pleasantries while Judith put the finishing touches on the meal. Several times she saw the lady look down at her watch and wondered if she had put herself on some kind of schedule.

At noon, when most of the preparations had been complete, Judith pulled off her apron. "Let's go have a glass of eggnog or wine before we eat."

When they stepped into the parlor, Harold looked up and put down the book he'd been reading. "Ladies, I'm glad you've joined me. Come on in."

The front doorbell rang as soon as Margaret seated herself on the couch facing the fireplace.

"I hope you don't mind," Judith said, "but I've invited a couple of people to eat. There's no way we can eat all this food alone."

Before Margaret could answer, she heard the familiar deep voice of Paul and the laugh of someone who had to be Joe. Her heart skipped a beat and a familiar warmth inched its way up her neck. She closed her eyes. *Oh, what a wonderful Christmas this will be.*

She was glad she'd taken the time to wash her hair and to dab on a little lipstick. When Paul stepped into the entranceway, her breath caught in her throat. For nearly two weeks, Paul had worn jeans, a work shirt, his red plaid jacket, and a cap on his head.

Today he stood just inside the door wearing a beautiful full-length wool coat. He placed a shopping bag on the floor, then pulled off his gloves and hat, all the time talking with Dr. Sabastian as easily as if he were one of the college faculty.

When he pulled off his coat, Margaret swallowed hard. He wore a pair of dark brown dress pants with a tweed sports coat covering a cream dress shirt opened at the collar. No clothes could camouflage the broad shoulders and muscular arms and legs, but today the rich attire emphasized a classiness that she hadn't recognized earlier.

Was this the same Paul Reynor who had hauled her wood just two weeks ago? When had this transformation taken place?

Joe followed him into the room. He, too, had dressed for Christmas dinner with his dress pants and thick blue sweater. In as many years as she'd been going to the park, she'd never seen Joe in anything but his tan park uniform. She smiled at his effort today.

With open arms, he walked right up to Margaret. "There's my girl. You had this old man worried." Joe bent down and hugged her.

She hugged him back and relished his fatherly warmth. "I'm so sorry I had everyone upset. I swear the ankle isn't bad at all. I think I'll be able to get back up to the cabin next week to finish out my vacation."

With one last quick hug, he let her go, but before he got up, Margaret detected a sniffle. "You do that. You tell that doctor that we'll make sure you stay put and do what you're told."

He got up, and Margaret introduced him to Judith Sabastian.

"Thank you, ma'am, for having us over. I can't wait to have a home-cooked meal, but mostly I missed our girl here."

Judith reached out and shook his hand in her usual friendly manner. "Well, you shouldn't have waited until today before coming. Our home is always open to Margaret's friends." She took his hand. "Come, let me fix you something to drink."

As they walked out of the room, Paul stepped in front of her. "You're looking better."

Margaret nodded dumbly, searching for her voice. "I'm feeling much, much better. As I just told Joe, I expect to be back at the cabin this week. I can get around pretty good now. I don't think I'll be able to manage those snow skis next week, but I know I'll be able to walk around the grounds a little." She was blabbering, but her nerves had taken control of her voice.

Paul walked in front of the couch and sat on the other end. "Good. Joe and I've already talked about getting you back up there. We can come get you as soon as you feel you're ready."

"Really? You'd drive back down the mountain again."

"Why, sure." He laughed deeply. "It's just a little mountain."

His gaiety was contagious and she laughed along with him. "I go back to the doctor tomorrow. Maybe he'll discharge me."

Joe, Judith, and Dr. Sabastian came back into the room carrying clear glass cups of warm cider. Judith spoke up. "We thought this cider would be nicer before dinner. We'll save the eggnog until after."

Paul stood up and took two cups and handed one to Margaret. "Sounds great."

Margaret felt the warmth all the way through her body, but it wasn't the heat from the cider. She let the warmth settle around her heart and for a second she fought a ball of emotion forming in her chest. This was Christmas, sitting around a fire, waiting to enjoy a meal of turkey and dressing with those that she loved. This is the way Christmas was supposed to feel.

As she looked around, she knew that she loved these people. Judith and Harold Sabastian had come to be so much more than a faculty acquaintance. Judith was like the mother she never had. Joe and Harold had both become substitute father figures.

Then her gaze settled on Paul. It worried her the way her heart fluttered each time she was near him. How could she possibly put him into the group with those that she loved? She'd only known him for two weeks, and even though she'd felt his lips on hers, she was afraid she was reading more into those few kisses than he was.

Anyway, how could she even think of another man in the same afternoon when she'd almost teared up thinking about Edward's last Christmas with her?

But as she listened to Paul talk with the Sabastians and joke around with Joe, she knew she had a lot to consider during the last two weeks of vacation. The more she was with Paul, the more she wanted to know about him.

As the others made their way into the dining room, Paul offered his hand to her. "Let's go join the others."

Margaret accepted his help. "Thanks, Paul. I feel so clumsy."

"There's a reason for that, young lady. You just got out of the hospital."

"Yes, I know, but it doesn't make it any easier to hobble around here like an invalid."

"You're not a total invalid. I'm not offering to carry you."

As soon as the words left his mouth, his gaze settled on her. Was he remembering how he'd carried her on the trail? Did he know how she felt as she'd held onto his neck and how she never wanted to ever let go?

Margaret took his hand then leaned into him as his arm encircled her. She wanted more than anything to snuggle against him, ignore the others in the house, and feel his lips on hers once more, but, of course, she couldn't.

"It's a good thing you're not having to carry me," she said, as she put as much weight on her ankle as it would allow and tried to walk without too much help. "I plan to eat a lot. I've been smelling Judith's cooking all morning."

"There're three men in the house. Eat all you want. We'll get you up the stairs one way or the other."

Paul sat next to her at the table, waited on her as if she were special, and smiled at her when no one else was looking. Except for the short exchange on their way to the dining room, they hadn't said much to each other all day. Maybe that was a sign that they didn't belong together or maybe it was a sign that words were not necessary.

When they headed back to the den to open gifts, Margaret let Paul help her to a chair. She did feel like an invalid now that she'd been out of the bed for so long. Her ankle had begun to throb once more.

By the time she reached the couch, she plopped down unceremoniously. "Whew. I made it."

Paul pulled an ottoman in front of her and lifted her foot on it. "Yep, you did, but that perspiration on your forehead tells me that maybe I should have carried you."

For a second Margaret felt as though the two of them were the only two in the room. His hands gently placed her foot on the cushion. His were large hands that she'd come to recognize as gentle and capable, hands that she wanted to reach out to hold.

Again, she did a mental shake of the head.

"That ought to do it," he said and winked at her. "Looks like you're getting some swelling. Do you think you ought to get back in bed?"

"No, no. I really want to stay down here with the rest of you."

When they all seated themselves in a circle, Margaret spoke up. "I just want all of you to know how special you are to me. Each one of you. All of you are like family to me." She looked over at Joe. "Did you go to my cabin and pick up my packages?"

"You told me to, didn't you?"

Everyone laughed. "Yes. I shouldn't have asked."

Judith acted first. She reached under the massive tree and pulled out a small gift and handed it to Margaret. She opened the first of several gifts from them that included things they knew she loved: homemade marmalade from a small country store, a small book of poetry, an audio from a lecture she had wanted to attend, but couldn't.

"Thank you so much," she said. "These are so special."

"Well," Joe humphed, "my gift ain't so fancy as that audio thing or book of poetry, but it'll warm you in that rocker you have at the cabin."

Margaret ripped the paper off a large box to find a beautiful afghan. "Oh, this is really lovely." She held it up to her face. "And so soft."

Joe beamed. "Barbara, Paul's friend at the restaurant, makes them and sells them during the holidays."

"I'll have to thank her personally."

It was her turn. She handed beautifully wrapped gifts to Dr. and Mrs. Sabastian and to Joe, people she'd always remembered at the holidays, but in her heart, she wished she had something for Paul as well. How was she to know there would be someone extra special left off her shopping list?

After everyone opened their gifts, Paul handed her a small box. She looked up and smiled. "Oh, Paul. I wish I had something for you." Her voice was low, only for his ears, then unwrapped the box carefully. First she found a book entitled *Wildlife of the Blue Ridge Mountains.*

"I thought you might like to name some of the creatures that come around the cabin." He hesitated then added, "And my house. There're lots of birds around there."

She flipped through the pages then held it to her chest. "This is great. Thank you." She then pushed the tissue away to find a CD of Christmas music.

"You never did get to see your carolers. Thought you might like to hear some of the music anyway."

She looked up and caught his gaze, and together they shared a moment that only the two of them understood. How long had it been that she and a man had had a conversation that only the two of them understood? For her, the moment and the gift were extra special.

Margaret handed the CD to Judith. "We can listen to some of it now, if you'd like."

She lifted her gaze back to Paul's. "Thank you." Her voice was soft, but what she really wanted to do was to thank him with a hug and a kiss, but that wouldn't be appropriate. Instead, she looked up. "Thanks to all of you. You've made this a wonderful Christmas for me."

By the time the rest of the presents were opened,

Margaret was too tired to walk anyone to the door. Aggravated at herself for being such a wimp, she said good-bye to Joe with a hug from the couch. Quickly he walked to the door followed by the Sabastians. They all disappeared into the sitting room across the hall.

Margaret was embarrassed, and she could tell that Paul was as well. He stuck his hands in his pockets. "Uh, I think they wanted me to say good-bye to you alone."

"It looks that way. I'm sorry. My friends seem to play matchmaker for me with any single man that comes to their door."

He chuckled, seemed to relax, then sat next to her on the couch. Without any more talking, he put his arm around her pulling her into his embrace. When his lips met hers, her body trembled. She extended her arms around his neck and kissed him back. For a long moment, she was lost in this man's warmth and strength and never wanted it to end.

But it did.

He pulled away and pushed a wisp of hair away from her forehead. "I'm glad we came down today. This was a good Christmas."

"Yes, it was. Thank you for coming. I was ready to have a pity party because I couldn't get out of the house, but you and Joe and the Sabastians made it a wonderful day."

He stood up, leaving her feeling cold and vulnerable and wanting his arms around her more than anything she'd wanted in a long, long time.

"It was wonderful," he said as he pulled his coat on. "I owe the Sabastians a lot for inviting us. Joe and I were going to spend it at the park."

"You aren't seeing your sister today?"

"No, not this year. They went down to her in-laws. They'll be back tonight."

For a moment he stood in silence. Their gazes locked, but neither said a word. Finally, he raised his hand and winked. "Behave yourself. You still have a couple weeks of vacation left."

As she watched him leave, she wished she had the courage to tell him how she felt.

## *Chapter Twelve*

The cabin's worn furniture and the big stone fireplace never looked so good as it did the day Margaret walked back in. *Walked* might have been stretching what she did, but she did manage to get from the truck to the cabin on her own using her crutches. Paul had driven down just as he'd said he would and drove her back up the mountain the day after Christmas.

Standing in the middle of the floor with his legs apart, he looked around the cabin. "Tell me what I can do for you before I leave."

"You've done enough. I have everything right here."

"I really hate to leave you, but I have a couple things to do before I get back to town."

Disappointment settled around her, but she let it

go. "I appreciate all you've done. I'm just glad to be here. I have my laptop here, your walkie-talkie, snacks, drinks. What else could I ask for?"

He hesitated. "Promise you'll use that walkie-talkie if you need Joe."

"I promise. Now go on before you're on the road until midnight. You don't want me to lie here and worry about you, do you?"

He pulled his gloves out of his pocket, but walked over to her bed before slipping them on. Margaret's breath caught in her throat knowing he wanted to kiss her good-bye.

Sitting on the edge of the mattress, he leaned over and placed his arms next to her head. "I haven't had anyone worry about me in a long time."

Margaret swallowed. "We make a good pair. I'll lie here worrying about you on the road, and you'll be on the road worrying about me lying here."

"Yeah, I guess that's kind of silly, huh?"

His face was next to hers. His breath warmed her face. "Yeah. Silly."

He bent down lower. She closed her eyes and waited for his kiss. How nice it would be to have him crawl into bed and to cuddle up next to him, but instead of feeling his kiss on her lips, he kissed her forehead, then stood up.

Her eyes flew open. How embarrassing. He hadn't meant to kiss her at all.

He slipped his hands into his gloves. "I hate leaving you here all alone. Sorry I have to go."

In spite of herself, Margaret's heart did a flop. "I don't want you to go, but . . ."

"Yep, there's always a *but* and tonight it's one I have to listen to."

He bent down and touched her nose with his finger. Not what she wanted him to do at all.

"I should be back early tomorrow. I'll come in and check on you. Joe said he'd ride up here as well, but promise—"

"I promise I'll call."

Lying perfectly still and feeling totally confused, she listened to him drive off. Seems she'd done a lot of that lately.

What had just happened? Where was the hint of romance that he'd shown her at the Sabastians? Was he afraid to kiss her alone in the cabin? Had he decided that kissing her wasn't the thing to do at all?

Had he come to his senses and decided that she wasn't the kind of woman that he'd want to get involved with?

"Oooh." She hit the mattress with her fist. "I finally let someone kiss me after three years and I blow it."

Paul pulled up to his driveway in the valley hardly remembering driving down the mountain. After leaving Margaret at the Sabastians on Christmas, he'd done some soul searching. He knew that Margaret was someone he could love. Maybe he was kidding himself. Maybe he loved her already.

That was the problem. Having his heart crushed once had been horrible. Margaret was different, and if he allowed himself to fall for her, the pain would be even worse.

Just because Margaret's image stayed with him long after he left her was no reason to forget who she was. And just because the feel of her lips had lingered on his for days was no reason to forget what her life was all about. Hers was a world of sophistication, intellect, and elite culture. His was a world of nature and simplicity. He appreciated those other things, but he didn't want to spend his life that way. Not again.

He felt sure if he encouraged a relationship, she would fall into his arms, but he also felt sure that a relationship with her would have him living next to the campus doing the things that were required of her career.

It wouldn't be fair to her to take her away from the things and the people she loved, but neither would it be fair to him to give up his dream.

He'd made up his mind. She was a guest at the park and that's all he would allow her to be—no matter how much more he wanted from her.

* * *

Margaret sat up straight in her rocker. The familiar crunching of snow and ice on the road outside announced that someone had pulled up to her cabin. Paul had said he'd come by to check on her, and now that he was here, her breath hitched and her heart beat in double-time.

With her leg propped up on an old ottoman and her laptop balanced in her lap, she'd tried to do something productive with her morning, but no matter how hard she tried, she hadn't made a lot of progress. She'd given up on her fiction writing, but there were pages and pages of notes to be made for her classes next semester. Even these lacked her standard professional enthusiasm.

And the job offer? Did she really want to seriously consider such a move? Would she enjoy the life on a huge university campus across the country?

She frowned. Since she'd come to the cabin, she hadn't given the offer the time it deserved. If she were honest with herself, she hadn't given thought about much else since Paul had walked up to her cabin door. She did know that somewhere since her trip up to the cabin, the move to the West Coast had lost its luster.

Today, there was no mistake as to why her brain wasn't functioning. As much as she hated to admit it, she'd been waiting for Paul to come by, and now as the truck door slammed outside her cabin, she ran her fingers through her hair and hoped she had some color back in her face.

With a quick knock and a turn of a key, the door opened.

"Margaret? It's me, Joe. Can I come in?"

Covering a wave of disappointment, she plastered a smile on her face. "Good morning, Joe. Come on in."

He closed the door behind him and stepped inside carrying a bag. He set it down on the corner countertop then came over and gave her a hug. "How're you doing this morning?"

"I'm doing great, but I'm ready to get this brace off so I can go outside again."

"Just be patient. Doc said you'd be up and running in no time." He nodded to the bag. "I had one of the other guys stop at the store before coming up this morning. Thought you might need a few more things."

"You're a doll, but I'm not sure who's going to eat all that food you and Paul brought up here before I go back."

Joe busied himself taking things out of the bag. "Well, for one, me. I'm going to fix us something and share your meal, if that's okay with you." He looked up with a frown.

"You know it is. I'm no fool. If someone wants to wait on me, I'm perfectly willing to sit and watch."

That brought a smile to his face.

Margaret relaxed against the back of the rocker, dying to know where Paul was. Had he not come to work today? Was he avoiding her?

Ouch, that last thought hurt. What if he was? What had she done to scare him away?

Joe was talking to her as he heated up something in the microwave and slapped together sandwiches. She tried to follow his train of thought but her own mind was flying from one reason to the next as to why Joe was here instead of Paul.

Joe's jabbering finally sunk in. "On top of Paul not being here, I'm in a little bit of a bind with this skeleton crew."

Margaret sat up straight. "Paul's not in today? Is he sick?"

"No, weren't you listening to me? I said he called me early this morning and told me that his sister had been in an accident, and he was heading across the state line to be with her and her family."

"Oh, my goodness. Is she hurt bad? Was it a car accident?"

He placed his hands on his hips. "I guess you really weren't listening. She was hit by another car. It slid right across an intersection on the ice."

Had he really said all that while she was daydreaming of Paul? "I'm sorry, Joe. My mind's still a little boggled."

"You got that right." He put the sandwiches on their

plates next to their bowls of canned stew, brought a tray over to her, then pulled a chair up for himself. "Maybe you had something else on your mind."

What she had on her mind was Paul, and she had no doubts that Joe knew that.

She stared at the food on her plate, though not really seeing it. "When does he plan to come back?"

Joe shrugged as he blew on a spoonful of stew. "Don't know. He sounded really upset. He did tell me to be sure to tell you where he was."

She nodded. A tiny bit of relief replaced the emptiness she had felt earlier.

Joe looked around the cabin. "I think by next tourist season we need to run some telephone lines out to all the cabins. People used to love the peace and quiet, but now, I don't know, things seem to happen all the time. The world's not like it used to be."

Margaret spoke up right away. "You're right. The world's changing." *And my world's coming unglued.*

Joe scratched his head. "I guess whether I like it or not, we'll have to move the park into the twenty-first century."

Margaret washed down a bite of sandwich with her drink. "I think telephones are important for security. We're all so used to being in contact with our cell phones that we get a little lost without a phone of any kind. I didn't know I was so dependent on one until I got up here."

Joe nodded. “I’ll see what I can do about getting the dab-burned things installed in each cabin.”

Margaret wondered if she’d be around to see the new development of bringing the cabins into the next century. Would she come back up here next Christmas or would she be on the other side of the continent in some concrete jungle?

And more importantly, would there be a reason to come back up here?

## *Chapter Thirteen*

Paul sat in yet another hospital waiting area hoping to hear something about his sister Ellen. The accident hadn't been a bad one, but the force of the impact slammed her head against the side of the car. Her husband, Raymond, had been taken in to see her over thirty minutes ago, and Paul had been sitting alone ever since.

It was the last thing he wanted to do. With nothing else to occupy his mind, his thoughts naturally settled on his sister and her husband and their children. Theirs was a perfect marriage, or so it seemed to him. He loved going over to their house to play with the two kids. He always left feeling happy for what his sister had found, but at the same time a little envious of what she had.

Raymond came down the hallway, pale with a strained grin. Paul stood up and reached for his hand when Raymond stepped near him. Without warning, Raymond collapsed on Paul's shoulder and sobbed.

"My God, what's the matter? I thought she was okay."

Raymond took a few minutes to catch his breath. "She is. She's going to be fine." He took out a handkerchief and wiped his nose. "I'm sorry. I just got so emotional thinking about what could have happened to her, I couldn't hold it back any more."

"Here, sit down. Tell me what the doctor said."

Paul led Raymond to a chair where he collapsed down. He explained about a concussion and a few abrasions, but all in all, Ellen was lucky. She'd be okay.

"Well, then we ought to celebrate," Paul said.

Raymond nodded, but sat still and stared at the floor. "You don't know what it's like to see the one you love lying on a stretcher. Thinking maybe you won't have her to spend the rest of your life with. Paul, I love your sister so much. She's my life."

Paul sat dumbfounded. He'd never seen Raymond show emotion of any kind, but as he watched his brother-in-law try to find some composure, he remembered what he'd felt when he'd seen Margaret lying helpless in the snow. Unlike Ellen and Raymond, he and Margaret had never made plans to spend the rest of their lives together. They'd never sat and dreamed together, but when he saw her in the snow, he knew that he wanted to do all those things with her.

How had he ever thought he could live without her?

"Paul, the most wonderful thing in the world is to share your life with someone. I worry about you, man. I worry you're letting your life go by because you're scared that you'll choose wrong."

Paul sat upright and held up his hands to his brother-in-law. "Hey, look, this conversation is supposed to be about my sister, not about me."

"Yeah, well, she worries about you too. What is it you're looking for? The perfect woman? The perfect mate? Well, let me tell you, there's no such thing. You work to make a good marriage, then she becomes the perfect mate."

Leaning against the back of the chair, Paul felt as though the air had been let out of him. "I don't know what I'm looking for. Maybe I'm not looking at all."

"You're not getting any younger, my man, and whatever it is you're looking for might not be real obvious. Sometimes looking for just the right thing isn't the way to go about your search."

Paul fidgeted in the chair. Is that what he'd been doing?

Then as if reading his mind, Raymond continued. "Your sister isn't perfect and neither am I, but we work at our marriage, and I can tell you, what we have is unbeatable. If something had happened to her today, I don't know what I would've done." He looked up at Paul. "Don't you ever pass up the opportunity to love someone like that."

Paul wondered if his brother-in-law knew he had touched on the right subject at just the right time. He watched him blow his nose.

"Did you know?"

Raymond crinkled his brow. "Did I know what?"

"Did you know Ellen was the perfect mate for you before you married her?"

"Not really. We had fun together. I liked being with her. That's all it was at first. Then I realized one day that I didn't want a day to go by without seeing her and knew that if I let her go, I'd be making a big, big mistake."

Paul understood. That's exactly how he felt on the days he couldn't see Margaret. Maybe he hadn't known her for very long, but they weren't kids anymore. He had to let her know that he wanted them to have a chance together, a chance for a lifetime together.

"I need to make a phone call. Will you be okay?"

"Yeah, they'll have Ellen in a room soon. Why don't you go on to the house? I want to stay up here with her."

Paul closed the door to his truck then reached for his cell phone. When Joe answered, he told him to go get Margaret up to the station so he could talk with her on the phone.

"Now?" Joe screeched into the phone. "You want me to go get her now?"

Paul looked at his watch. "It's only five. Come on, Joe. I need to tell her something."

He listened to Joe grumble, then say he'd have her at the cabin in about thirty minutes. "That'll give the poor woman some time to change clothes. She's probably already in her night clothes."

"I doubt that, but I'll give you thirty minutes."

He started the truck and drove through town keeping an eye on the time. Before he reached his sister's house he pulled off the road and parked.

As he listened to the telephone ring in the office, his insides tightened. What is it he was about to tell this woman? Maybe this was a mistake.

"Hello." It was Margaret's voice, not Joe's as he was expecting.

"Margaret, is that you?"

"Yes. Paul, is something wrong? Is your sister okay?"

Glad to have something to talk about besides why he called, he told her about his sister's accident.

"I'm so glad. You had me worried."

There was a lull. Paul swallowed.

"Margaret, I'm sorry I had Joe drag you down to the phone, but I wanted to talk with you. I, uh, left pretty abruptly the other day. I didn't want to leave you with the wrong impression."

"The wrong impression?"

His mind was spinning. He was blowing it. "Uh, I have a feeling you thought I left mad or something." He stopped, knowing how ridiculous he was sounding. "Look, maybe I shouldn't have called. I'm not sure what it is I wanted to tell you."

Her voice was soft when she answered. "Paul, talk to me. I'm glad you called. What I thought when you left was that you were upset with me. Did I do something wrong?"

"No, no," he answered into the phone and closed his eyes. "No, you didn't do anything wrong. I got scared. Don't laugh," he said quickly, "but I scared myself. We've only known each other for a couple of weeks and we—I—was moving pretty fast."

He waited for her to answer. He could hear her breathing, but she said nothing.

"Margaret, are you still there?"

"Yes. I'm still here. I guess you took me a little off guard just now, but if it makes you feel any better, I didn't notice that you were moving too fast. I'm a little out of practice at this dating game." Her voice dropped, "If that's what we were doing. I was a little hesitant at first, but I thought we were having fun together."

Paul let out a long breath he'd been holding. "Me

too. I was having fun with you. I like being around you, and that's what I was calling to tell you. I miss not seeing you since I'm up here. I miss not being able to stop by your cabin to say hello and standing on your stoop talking to you. I miss you period and I want to do something about that."

There was a long silence before he continued. "I, I guess I needed to let you know."

Another long silence. Paul's forehead broke out in a sweat before she finally answered him.

"I'm glad you called. We have a lot to talk about, but I think we can wait until I see you again. Do you think you'll get back up here before I go back to campus?"

"Oh yeah, if I have anything to do with it. I've got to help my brother-in-law out for a little while, but I'll be back in a couple of days."

He asked her about her leg, feeling now as if the words flowed more freely. He had told her he missed her, and she was glad he'd called.

Maybe he'd done something right.

For the next two days, Paul helped with the kids so that Raymond could spend as much time with Ellen at the hospital as possible, but as soon she was discharged, Paul couldn't get back on the interstate fast enough.

He didn't go directly up the mountain though. There was something else he needed to do.

Instead, he headed for the Sabastians.

* * *

After the phone call from Paul, Margaret settled into her quiet days in the cabin, concentrating on getting her ankle better and trying to decipher her feelings and periodically thinking about the new job offer.

The more she thought about leaving this area, the more she convinced herself that the new position was not for her. A bigger salary in a new town couldn't offer her any more than she had right here. Making up her mind, she'd call the Sabastians tomorrow to let them know she was staying on.

With that problem out of the way, she tried to write, but it did no good. She finally gave up on that idea and spent her afternoons walking near the cabin or sitting in a chair right outside the door. By nightfall she'd collapse in her rocker with a book.

There was so much to think about. Paul's telephone call had added a mix to the cauldron of emotions she stirred.

Coming up to the mountain had been her way of coping with the holidays, but this year something totally unexpected had happened to her. She now understood this retreat had become her way of hiding from the world, and she was tired of hiding.

She didn't know what was ahead for her, but she knew she was ready to start living again. Tonight as she sat in her rocker holding her unread book, she watched the flames dance in the fireplace. There was so much to think about.

Just sitting in the dim light of the cabin pulled her into the quiet world to which she and Edward had become accustomed. "Oh, Edward, can you forgive me if I don't come up here alone again? You know I'll always love you, but I need to move on, and there's a man out there that might be able to show me the way."

There was no sadness as she said the words. In fact, she smiled, remembering how that fire had warmed their love and helped it to grow. Edward's gift to her had been the opening of a door to the world that had been too heavy for her to move. Now that door swung open easily and she was ready to walk through it. She dared to hope that Paul would be there by her.

She sat in the rocker for a long time remembering and reliving and storing away each memory of her former marriage. They'd live with her forever.

As she reveled in her determination to leave her emotional door open for Paul, noises outside of the cabin startled her. Holding her breath, she placed the book in her lap and listened. Bears? Could it be bears in the middle of winter?

She shook her head.

Intruders? No, never. Not here in her park.

Out of the quietness of the evening came the sounds of singing. Her first glance was to the CD player, but it was off. Cautiously, she walked to the window. In the blackness of the mountain night, one small circle of light shone down from a kerosene lantern hung from a tree limb.

She blinked and looked closely. Under the lantern stood a little group of carolers bundled up against the mountain cold: Joe, Barbara and David from the café, Dr. and Mrs. Sabastian, another park ranger, and Paul.

Tears flooded her eyes. She hadn't seen carolers in years. Hadn't needed or wanted carolers. Tonight was different. Christmas night might be over, but the season was still upon her.

Brushing away the tears, she donned her heavy coat, then hurried out to listen to the music.

Her gaze met Paul's. He winked then looked up at the light. It wasn't a fancy, high-tech streetlight, but the tiny light from its flame cut through her darkness as nothing else had done in years.

Swallowing the knot of emotion in her throat, she returned Paul's wink and sat on the stoop.

She had come to the mountains to escape the holidays, but a man in a red plaid jacket had brought the holiday cheer to her. She was ready to embrace it, and in her heart she knew she was ready for a lot of other things as well.

Paul Reynor was at the top of her list.